# Perfect. That's what she was.

William stru is chest. Never graceful way over a fragile itself. Feeling

She glowed with happiness as she headed his way. "I've been wanting to do more rain chimes, with the fall rains a few months away. This will be perfect."

"Rain chimes? Never heard of them."

"You'll get the first one for the season. They're like wind chimes, but instead of wind, they catch the rain and chime."

He could see the way she took the ordinary and made it a little lovelier. They had that in common, the appreciation of what was right in front of them. She broke down his reserve and he felt revealed as the warm mountain breeze swept over him. Aubrey came close, but he didn't move away.

**Books by Jillian Hart**

Steeple Hill Love Inspired

*Heaven Sent* #143
*\*His Hometown Girl* #180
*A Love Worth Waiting For* #203
*Heaven Knows* #212
*\*The Sweetest Gift* #243
*\*Heart and Soul* #251
*\*Almost Heaven* #260
*\*Holiday Homecoming* #272
*\*Sweet Blessings* #295
*For the Twins' Sake* #308
*\*Heaven's Touch* #315
*\*Blessed Vows* #327
*\*A Handful of Heaven* #335
*\*A Soldier for Christmas* #367
*\*Precious Blessings* #383
*\*Every Kind of Heaven* #387
*\*Everyday Blessings* #400

\*The McKaslin Clan

## *JILLIAN HART*

makes her home in Washington State, where she has lived most of her life. When Jillian is not hard at work on her next story, she loves to read, go to lunch with her friends and spend quiet evenings with her family.

# Jillian Hart
## Everyday Blessings

Steeple
Hill®

Published by Steeple Hill Books™

STEEPLE HILL BOOKS

Steeple
Hill®

ISBN-13: 978-0-373-81314-8
ISBN-10:    0-373-81314-7

EVERYDAY BLESSINGS

www.SteepleHill.com

Printed in U.S.A.

Put on a heart of compassion.
—*Colossians* 3:12

# Chapter One

Aubrey McKaslin didn't know if she was coming or going. All she knew was that her eighteen-month-old niece was crying in agony, holding her fists to her ears. The little girl's cries echoed in the coved ceiling of the dining nook of her stepsister Danielle's home. To top it off, her almost five-year-old nephew Tyler was refusing to eat his dinner.

She was running on four hours' sleep at the end of a difficult day that came at the end of a very bad week, and she was at her wit's end. And she wasn't the only one. Tyler, always a good and dependable boy, gave his plate a push away from him at the table and shot her a mulish glare.

"I want Mommy. I don't want Mexi-fries!" He choked back a sob, his eyes full of pain. "I want my d-daddy. I want him to come h-home."

"I know, but he can't come, pumpkin. He's still in the hospital." Aubrey ran a loving hand over his tousled head. "You know he would be here with you if he could."

"But why?"

"Because he's sick, honey." Aubrey's heart broke as she bounced the weepy little girl on her hip, to comfort her. With her free hand, she knelt to brush her fingertips down the little boy's nose. It usually made him smile, but not this evening. No, it had been a rough day for all of them.

On days like this, she wanted to know why so many hardships. She'd take it to the Lord in prayer, but she knew that life was like this, sometimes difficult, sometimes beyond understanding. All she could do was make the best of such an awful day.

"But why's he sick?" Fat tears glistened in Tyler's sorrowful eyes. "Why?"

Tyler's dad, Jonas, wasn't sick. He'd

slipped into a degenerating coma, as the doctor had told them this afternoon. Jonas was a state trooper who'd been shot ten days ago when he'd stopped a speeder, who apparently had an outstanding warrant for his arrest and didn't want to be caught. The man was still at large.

"When I'm sick, I hafta stay in bed or quiet on the couch." The boy's soulful eyes were filled with such innocence. "Daddy can, too?"

How could she explain this to him so he'd understand? Aubrey was at a loss. She loved her nephew; in the end, that's all she could do for him. Love him through his pain. "Your daddy is so sick he has to stay at the hospital."

"N-no?" Tyler choked on a sob. "I w-want my da-daddy. He's gotta have M-Mexi-fries."

So, that's what this was about. She'd picked up fast-food Mexican meals on her way here to take turns sitting with the kids. Aubrey knew now why Tyler was so upset. It was a standing jest in the family that Mexi-fries, which were seasoned, deep-fried Tater Tots from a local taco place, could solve a host of problems. Being sick was one of them. "How about I ask your aunt Ava to take care of that? Will that make you feel better?"

"Y-yes." Tyler was sobbing so hard he choked.

Poor little boy. Aubrey's heart broke all over again for him as she wrapped her free arm around him. He clung to her, crying as hard as the baby in her other arm. How their mother handled this on a daily basis, Aubrey didn't know. Talk about a tough job.

But an important one. A job she'd given up hope on ever having as her own considering the way her life was going. She pressed a kiss to Tyler's temple. "Are you feeling better now?"

"Y-yeah." He hiccupped and let go to rub his tears away with his fists. "I'm a big boy."

"Yes, you are. A very big boy. You're doing a terrific job, champ."

"Y-yeah." He gave a sniff and stared at his plate. "Do I gotta eat the Mexi-fries?"

"Try to eat something, okay?" She rubbed her free hand over Madison's soft, downy head. The antibiotics she'd picked up earlier hadn't kicked in yet, or at least not enough, and she was still in misery. "I'm going to try rocking her again. I'll be right over here if you need me."

"O-kay." Tyler hiccupped again, wrestling down his own misery, and stared halfheartedly at his plate.

Madison wrapped her little fists in Aubrey's long blond hair and yanked, at the same time burying her face in Aubrey's neck.

Poor baby. Aubrey began humming a Christian pop tune, the first thing that came into her head as she ambled over to the rocker in the corner of the living room. The instant she sank onto the soft cushion, Madison let out a scream of protest. She must be missing her mom, too.

"It's all right, baby," she soothed, and Madison's cries became sobs.

*Lord, please show me how to help them, how to comfort them.* She closed her eyes and prayed with all her heart, but no answer seemed to come as the air conditioner kicked on, breezing cool air against her ankle.

Life had been so dark the past week and a half that she'd forgotten there was a beautiful, bright world outside the house. It was a gorgeous summer evening. The trees were in full bloom. Thick streams of sunshine tumbled through the dancing green leaves of the young maple trees in the backyard and glinted over the sparkling surface of the in-ground pool. The tabby cat stalked through the shadows of the perimeter shrubbery, and Danielle's flower baskets on the deck shivered cheerfully in the warm night breezes.

How could such a beautiful day hold so much sorrow?

Her cell began to chime, startling Madison even more. Red faced, the little girl slumped like a rag doll against Aubrey in defeat, her fingers fisting in the knit of Aubrey's summery top. She leaned her cheek against the little girl, willing as much comfort into her as she could while at the same time inching the phone out of her front shorts pocket. She checked the screen, just in case it was a call from family.

Ava's cell number came up—her twin

sister. Thank God for small miracles. "Tell me that you're on your way over. Please."

"Sorry, I wish I could." Ava's voice sounded thin and wavering, and Aubrey's stomach squeezed in a painful zing of sympathy. She knew what was coming before her twin said it. "Things aren't good here. Danielle's not okay. That's her husband in there, dying, and I can't leave her. Is that Madison?"

"You can hear her, huh?" No big surprise there. Aubrey kept the rocker moving and tried to comfort the baby, but things were just getting worse. Now Tyler was sobbing quietly at the table. "Have you heard if Dad and Dorrie's plane has landed yet?"

"No, but when they get here, I'll race straight over to give you a hand with the munchkins."

"Thanks, I'll take whatever help I can get."

"I'll hopefully see you soon and, in the meantime, I'll send a few prayers of help your way."

"Great, I'll take 'em."

The doorbell rang, the sound a pleasant

chime echoing in the high cathedral ceilings overhead. Tyler looked up, tears staining his face. Madison ignored it, keeping her face buried in Aubrey's neck. It was probably a thoughtful church member dropping by another casserole. "I gotta go. Someone's at the door."

"Who?"

"How can I tell? I'm not near the door. It's not family, because they would walk right in." Somehow she managed to straighten out of the chair without jostling Madison or dropping her cell phone. "Call me if anything changes, okay?"

That was all she could say with Tyler listening, all ears, trying to figure out what was really going on. But he was too little to understand, and overhearing it was not the right way to explain what was happening with his daddy.

"Understood," Ava said. "The doctor is talking with Danielle right now, so I'll let you know."

Aubrey flipped her phone shut. The doorbell pealed again, but she wasn't moving very fast. Neither was Tyler.

He slid off his seat and landed with a two-footed thud on the linoleum floor. He rubbed the tears away with his fists, smearing them across his pale cheeks. "I can get the door, Aunt Aubrey. I do it for Mom all the time."

"Go ahead, tiger." She followed him through the hallway to the front door, where the door's arched window gave her a good view of the newcomer standing on the porch. She caught the impression of a tall man with jet-black hair framing a stony face before Tyler wrenched the door open.

"Who're you?" he asked with a sniffle.

Aubrey stood up behind the boy, staring at the stranger who took one look at them and rechecked the house number tacked on the beige siding.

"I'm looking for Jonas Lowell." The man said in a gravelly baritone. "Do I have the right place?"

He had dark eyes that met her gaze like an electrical shock. He had an intense presence, not dark and not frightening, just solid. Like a man who knew his strength and his capability.

Aubrey couldn't find her voice, so she nodded, aware of Madison's baby-fine curls against her chin, the warm weight of the toddler, and the blast of dry summer wind on her face.

Tyler leaned against her knee, tipping his head all the way back to look at up at the man. "You're real tall. Are you a fireman?"

"No." The man came forward, and with the sun at his back shadowing him as he approached, he looked immense. His dark gaze intensified on hers. "You're not Danielle, right?"

"No, I'm her stepsister." He definitely was not a close friend of Jonas's, Aubrey decided. But there were friends who still didn't know. She opened the door wider. Not a lot of crime happened in this part of Montana, in spite of what had happened to Jonas.

"Maybe you didn't hear, I…" She paused. How did she find the words to say what had happened, with Tyler listening so intently? Danielle hadn't wanted him to know the whole truth yet. It was so violent and cruel. *Too* violent and cruel.

"I'm sorry to show up like this," the big man apologized. "I've left a few messages on Jonas's voice mail, but he hasn't gotten back to me."

"No, he's not going to be able to do that right now. He's in the hospital. If you want, I can have Danielle give you a call to explain." That might be best. Tyler was frightened enough as it was. She could feel his little body tense up, board-stiff against her knees.

"In the hospital?" The man looked stricken. "I'm sorry. I didn't know. You said you're Danielle's sister?"

"Yes, I'm Aubrey. Let me get a pen so I can get your number." It was hard to concentrate with Madison sobbing. She was gently rubbing the toddler's shoulder blades with her free hand. "Tyler, would you run and get a pen and the notepad by the phone for me?"

"Wait—" The man's rough baritone boomed like thunder. "Obviously this isn't a good time. I'm sorry for intruding. I'll leave my card with the gift—"

"Gift?" Okay, call her confused. She had no idea who this man was or what he was talking about. "I'm sorry. Run that by me again."

"Sure. Jonas bought a gift for his wife. An anniversary present. He was going to come by and pick it up, but since I hadn't heard from him, I thought I'd bring it by. Where do you want it?"

She felt her jaw dropping. Her heart cinched so tightly there was no possible way it could beat. "An anniversary gift? For Danielle?"

The man nodded warily, watching her closely as if he were afraid she was going to burst into tears or show some emotional reaction. Maybe it was his size, or the awkward way he'd taken a step back, but he seemed like the type who was easily panicked by an emotionally distraught woman.

Not that she was emotionally distraught. Yet. "If you could put it in the garage, maybe? I'll hit the opener for you. I'm sorry," she said as Madison began a more intense wave of crying. "This is really a bad time."

"I see that." He studied the little girl, his ruggedly handsome face lined with concern.

"It's an ear infection. The medicine's starting to work. I just have to rock her until she falls asleep."

"Alright, then." Stiffly, he took a step back. "Is Jonas going to be okay?"

No. But could she say that in front of Tyler? All she could do was shrug her shoulder. Tyler had frozen in place, ears peeled, eyes wide, trying to absorb any detail.

As if the stranger had noticed, he nodded in understanding. Sadness crossed his granite face. With a single nod, he turned and strode down the walkway, taking the shadows with him.

Immeasurably sad, Aubrey closed the door and sent Tyler into the garage to hit the button that activated the door opener. Madison was crying anew and there was nothing Aubrey could do but rock her gently back and forth, quietly singing the only song that came into her mind.

She wasn't even sure if she had the words right, because all she could think about was Jonas. Thoughtful Jonas. He'd gotten an anniversary gift for his wife, but would it become like a message from the grave? A final goodbye? Aubrey choked back her own sorrow. It was too horrible to think about.

Life could knock your feet out from under you with a moment's notice, she thought. You could have it all, do everything right, pray diligently and live your faith, and tragedy could still happen.

She tightened her arms around the little girl who might have to grow up without her daddy, and she tried not to wonder what awaited her family, the people she loved.

William Corey could see the woman— Aubrey—through the garden window. His opinion of women was shaky these days, due to his experience with the gender. But he could see how this woman was different.

Maybe it was the soft, thick, golden fall of sunlight through the glass that diffused the scene, like a filter on a camera's lens. That soft brush of opalescent light touched her blond hair and the porcelain curve of her heart-shaped face, making her look like rare goodness.

Or, maybe it was the child in her arms, clinging to her with total trust and need. Whatever the reason, she looked like innocence, pure and sweet.

Stop staring at the woman, William, he told himself and shook his head to clear away all thoughts of her. He popped the crew-cab door of his truck. Sweat dampened the collar of his T-shirt and the black knit clung to his shoulders as he lifted the wrapped frame from his rig. Across the street, a miniature dachshund came racing down from its front porch to bark and snarl, teeth snapping. It halted at the edge of the curb, glaring at him with black beady eyes. Someone shouted for it to shush and the little fellow kept barking, intent on driving William away.

"Yeah, I know how you feel, buddy," he said to the dog, who only barked harder in outrage. William didn't like strangers, either. He'd learned how to chase them with off with a few gruff words, too.

As he circled around to the open garage, he caught sight of the woman in the window, framed by the honeyed sheen of the kitchen cabinets. Washed with light, caught in the act of kissing the little toddler's downy head in comfort, she looked picture perfect.

His fingers itched for his camera to capture the moment, to play with light and angle and reveal this pure moment of tenderness. It had been a long time since he'd felt this need to work—since Kylie's death. It took all his will to drag his gaze from the kitchen window and force his thoughts away from the woman. His days of holding a camera in his hands were over.

"So, mister." The boy stood in the open inner door between the garage and the house, a lean, leggy little guy with too-big Bermuda shorts and a shocking-green tank top. His brown hair stuck straight up as if he'd been struck by lightning. Tear tracks stained his sun-browned cheeks and had dampened his eyelashes. "That's a present, huh?"

"For your mom." William softened the gruffness in his voice. He liked little kids, and he figured this one had enough hardship to deal with.

He leaned the framed photograph, carefully wrapped, against the inside wall safely away from the garbage cans and the lawn mower. "I'll just leave it here, alright? You make sure your mom gets it, okay? With all you've got going on in your family, it might be easy to forget this is here."

"I never forget nuthin'." The little boy said with a trembling lip. He gave a sigh that was part sob, sounding as if he were doing his best to hold back more tears. "My daddy's sick in the hospital."

"I'm real sorry about that."

"Me, too." The kid sniffed once.

William had questions, but he didn't know exactly what to ask. An illness? That didn't seem right; Jonas was the type of guy to hit the gym three times a week without fail. Not that William knew him well.

The little boy looked so lost, holding on to the doorknob with one hand, as if he were hanging on for dear life. What on earth should he say to him?

William stood in the shadows of the garage, as still as the boy, feeling big and awkward and lost. He'd been alone too long, out of the world so long that he wasn't used to making small talk with adults, much less a little boy.

"I miss my daddy. You haven't seen him, have ya?"

"No. Sorry." William could feel the kid's pain—it seemed to vibrate in the scorching heat. The silence stretched until it echoed in the empty rafters overhead. "How long has he been in the hospital?"

"A l-long time." The boy scrubbed his left eye with his free hand. "For-ev-ever."

William had a bad feeling about this, a strange reeling sense of the present lapping backward onto the past. "How old are you, kid?"

"I'm gonna be this much." He held up his whole hand. "Daddy'll be well, cuz he's takin' me to the f-fair. He prom-mised."

William studied the fat gleam of two silver tears spilling down the boy's cheeks and felt the sorrow of his own past. Things didn't always turn out well, stories didn't always end happily, and ill loved ones didn't always recover.

Maybe that wouldn't be the case for Jonas.

Faintly, from inside the house, came the woman's—Aubrey's—voice. "Tyler, close the garage door and come try to finish your supper, okay?"

Tyler hung his head and didn't answer. His pain was as palpable as the shadows creeping into the garage and the heat in the July air.

"You'd better go," William said, ambling toward the cement driveway, where birdsong lulled and leaves lazed in the hot breeze and the dog across the street was still yapping with protective diligence.

"Mister?"

The little boy's voice drew him back. William stilled. Even his heart seemed to stop beating.

"You could p-pray for my daddy so he can come ho-me." Tyler scrubbed his eyes again, took a step back and closed the inner door.

Leaving William alone in the heat and the shadows with an ache in his chest that would not stop.

## Chapter Two

Aubrey breathed a sigh of relief when she saw the inside door snap shut and Tyler plod across the linoleum. One problem down, and now she'd move to solving the next.

"Just eat something," she said softly to him, brushing her fingertips through his hair as he wove past her.

"Okay," he said on a sigh and halfheartedly climbed back up onto his chair.

Madison gave a hiccup and relaxed a little more. Good. Aubrey stood in place in the center on the kitchen, gently rocking back and forth, shifting her weight from her right foot to her left. The stinging tracer of pain fired down her left femur, as it always did when her leg was tired, but Aubrey didn't let that stop her, since Madison's breathing had begun to slow. She became as limp as a rag doll. Her fingers released Aubrey's shirt, so the collar was no longer digging into her throat.

Aubrey sent a prayer of thanks winging heavenward and pressed another kiss into the baby's crown of fine curls. Somewhere outside came the growl of a lawn mower roaring to life. Aubrey didn't know if it was cruel or comforting that the world kept on turning in the midst of a tragedy. That lawns still needed to be mowed and housework done. The gift Jonas had ordered for Danielle—now *that* was getting to her. She tried to swallow down the hot tears balling up in her throat.

The lawn mower was awfully loud. Either that, or awfully close. Aubrey eased forward a few steps to peer outside, careful not to disturb the sleeping toddler in her arms. The lawn had gone unmowed. Since everyone in the family was so busy juggling kid care and sitting with Danielle at the hospital, there wasn't any time left over for much else.

Not that she minded at all, but she hadn't been to the stables to ride her horse or able to work on her ceramics in her studio. There hadn't been time for normal living—only working at the bookstore and helping Danielle out afterward. But now that her dad and stepmom were flying in, they wouldn't all be stretched so thin.

Then she saw him. William. He was wrestling with the mower at the far end of the lawn, lining it up for the next pass. Dappled sunlight gilded his strong profile and broad shoulders as he guided the mower out of sight. For a moment she didn't believe her eyes. He was mowing the lawn?

She *knew* he was, and yet her mind sort of spun around as if it was stuck in neutral. She could only gape speechlessly at the two strips of mowed lawn, proof of a stranger's kindness. A tangible assurance, small but much needed, that God's goodness was at work. Always.

Don't worry, Aubrey, she told herself. This will work out, too.

She took a deep breath, watched William

stride back into her sight, easily pushing the mower in front of him, and she knew what she had to do.

William wiped at the gritty sweat with his arm, but it still trickled into his eyes and burned. He upended the final, full lawn-mower bag into the garage waste bin. It was hot, and although the sun was sinking low in its sky, the temperature felt hotter than ever.

All he wanted was to get into his rig, turn on the air-conditioning full blast and stop by the first convenience store for a cold bottle of water. He gave the heavy bag a shake to make sure all the cut grass was out and a dust cloud of tiny bits of grass and seed puffed into his face. He coughed, and the tiny grit stuck to his sweat-dampened skin. *This* was why he had a riding mower, not that it would be practical for Jonas's patch of lawn.

Jonas. In the hospital. It had to be an extended stay, since William had been leaving messages for the past week and a half or so. Which meant it was a serious deal. Sick at heart, William reattached the bag to the mower and wheeled it against the far wall, out of the way. Every movement echoed around him in the carless garage. There was the photograph, wrapped and propped carefully against the wall. The photograph he'd sold to Jonas for practically nothing.

He closed his eyes, and there was the memory, as vivid as real life. Jonas grinning, still in his trooper's uniform after a long shift. He was standing in front of the Gray Stone Church, where the united church charities in the valley met for their monthly meetings. He'd produced a hardback book of William's photographs for his signature.

"I really appreciate this, Will," Jonas had said in all sincerity. "My wife loves your work. It's a gift for our anniversary. It'll be seven years."

"Seven years," William had said while he'd scribbled his signature on the title page. "Isn't that said to be one of the most critical years?"

"Sure, I've heard of folks talking about the seven-year itch or whatever, but I don't get it. I've got the best wife in the world."

William had remembered, because he'd believed Jonas. The man had actually planned for his wedding anniversary a month in advance. He'd been telling the truth about his feelings for his wife. That was rare, in Will's opinion. After all, he knew. Once, the blessing of marriage had happened to him.

Maybe that's why he'd offered one of the photographs from his personal stash. He liked to think that the things he'd lost in life still existed somewhere. That there was a reason to hope, although he'd lost that hope right along with his faith, and a lot of other things.

Standing in the baking heat of Jonas's garage, William pulled out his wallet and searched through it until he found a battered business card, which he tucked around the string that held the brown paper wrapping in place. He thought of the little boy's sorrow, his request for prayer, and vowed to honor that request tonight. It had been a long time since he'd said a nightly prayer.

As he turned to go, the inside door opened. The sister—Aubrey—stood framed in the doorway, one slender hand on the doorknob, poised in midstep. She hesitated, as if she were a little shy, and she made a lovely picture with the child asleep in her arms.

The painful lump was back in his throat. A ghost of memory tried to haunt him, but he wrestled it down. The trick was to keep your heart rock hard.

"Oh, good. I'm glad I caught you," she said in a voice as soft as grace. "It's ninety-six degrees out there in the shade. I have a bottle of cold water, or lemonade. I didn't know which you'd prefer."

Sure enough, she'd managed to wrap her fingers awkwardly around two plastic bottles, and still cradled the sleeping baby lovingly against her.

"Water's fine." Somehow he got the words out.

"Thank you for doing this." She stopped to deposit one of the bottles out of sight and breezed toward him with a careful step. "You have no idea how much we appreciate it. You must be a good friend of Jonas's."

"He's a good man." William glanced behind her at the open door, knowing his voice might carry to the little boy inside. "I didn't know he was sick."

"He's not. That was the best way to explain to Tyler." Her answer came quietly. "He was shot on duty."

While it hadn't occurred to him, the possibility had been there, in the back of his mind, William realized.

"He was doing better, but he suffered something like a stroke a few days ago and now he's in a deep coma."

"Not good."

"No." Pain marked her face and weighed down that single word. She said nothing more.

She didn't have to. He knew too much about comas. Wished he didn't. "Is there anything more I can do for his family?"

"Prayer. God's grace is the only thing that will help him now."

What could he say to that? It was the truth, and from his experience, a deep coma was a death sentence. William moved forward to take the bottle of water she offered. He tried not to brush her fingers with his or to notice the stunning violet-blue of her eyes or the shadows within them. He would not let himself think too much on the soft feminine scents of shampoo and vanilla-scented lotion or her loveliness. It wasn't something he ordinarily noticed anymore.

"Thanks." He held up the bottle, ice-cold from the refrigerator, and kept moving. "Be sure and turn on the sprinkler after I leave. Oh, and I left my number with the package. If his condition changes, will you call me? Leave a message on my machine?"

"Yes, I will. Thank you again."

He didn't look back or acknowledge her as he strode straight to his vehicle, all business, and climbed in. He didn't look at her as he backed into the residential street or lift a hand in a goodbye wave as he drove away.

Aubrey watched the gleam of his tail-lights in the gathering twilight and couldn't help wondering who was this Good Samaritan? He hadn't exactly been friendly, but clearly he'd thought enough of Jonas to have pitched in with the lawn mowing.

He seemed distant and not exactly friendly. She felt as if she'd seen him some- where before, like in church or in the book- store her family ran. The look of him was familiar—though not the personality he radiated. That hard steel and sorrow would be memorable.

At a loss to explain it, she went to hit the button to close the garage door and noticed the bright yellow SUV whipping down the curve of the cul-de-sac and into the driveway. Behind the sheen of the sinking sun on the tinted windshield, she could see the faint image of her twin sister busily pulling the e-brake, turning off the engine and gathering her things, talking animat- edly as she went, which meant she had to be yakking on her cell phone.

Aubrey kept an ear to the open inside door, where she could hear the drone of the cartoon version of *A Christmas Carol* that Tyler watched over and over again. Knowing he was safely riveted in front of the television, she waited as the bright yellow driver's-side door swung open and Ava emerged. Her sister Ava was chaos as usual, her enormous purse slung over her shoulder, thick and bulky and banging her painfully in the hip. Yep, she was definitely on her cell, and judging by her shining happiness, she was talking to her handsome fiancé, Brice.

Madison stirred drowsily between wakefulness and sleep, and Aubrey patted her back gently and returned to rocking again. She watched as her sister gave her a welcoming wave, shut her SUV's door, then opened it and extracted her keys from the ignition.

"Oops." Ava grinned, keeping her voice quiet as she shut the door. "You've got Madison half-asleep."

"Working on it." Aubrey kept rocking, full of questions that would have to wait for later, she thought. Even if Tyler was momentarily distracted, any long discussion would have the little boy hurrying to come listen. But not all of her questions had to wait. "I take it that Dad and Dorrie are with Dani?"

"Yep, so the rest of us figured we'd let the parents stay with Danielle through the night, and we'll take turns relieving them tomorrow." Ava dragged her feet in exhaustion as she came closer. "Brice said he can take the kids in the morning, so at least that's taken care of."

"See? I told you. You've got a great guy."

"He's the best guy." She said it with confidence, as if she no longer had a single doubt.

And why would she? Brice was absolutely perfect. Happiness for her sister warred with the sadness she felt for her family and the odd aching sorrow that William left behind. Which reminded her. "Do you know a friend of Jonas's named William?"

"Nope. Then again, why would I? I can't keep my own name straight some days." Ava rolled her eyes and leaned close to reach for Madison. She transferred the sleepy child into her arms. "I'm taking over. You're officially off duty."

"When it comes to family, there no such thing as off duty."

"Stop being stubborn and go home—"

"To an empty apartment?"

For a moment they both paused in their lifelong habit of interrupting each other and finishing the other's sentences. Aubrey knew what Ava stopped short of saying. They'd spent their whole lives together. Even when they'd pursued different career paths after high school, they'd still been practically attached at the hip.

They talked throughout the day, all day long, thanks to the invention of cell phones. They met for lunch and dinner, and they shared an apartment. They spent their free time together as they always had. But Ava's marriage would change that.

Aubrey loved her sister with all her heart, and there was nothing more important than her happiness, but she knew she was going to miss spending so much time with her twin. When she looked into the future, Ava would have a home and a husband, children. That's where her time and energy should lie. Absolutely. But all Aubrey saw for herself was a long stretch of lonely evenings and weekends. Even now, without Madison in her arms, she felt lonely.

Not that she was going to be sad for herself for a second, because look at all the wonderful blessings the Lord put into her life with each and every day. But still, it was a change. And a big one.

"Tyler's watching one of his DVDs," she said with the most cheerful voice she could muster under the circumstances. "Maybe I'll just crash with him on the couch."

"Hey, what's that?" Nothing got past Ava. She pointed with her free hand to the wrapped gift.

"No idea. That William guy I mentioned dropped it off. It's an anniversary gift from Jonas to Danielle."

Ava looked sucker punched. "That's just about the saddest thing I've heard today, and it's been a day with a whole lot of sad in it."

"Tell me about it," she said over the sound of the garage door ratcheting closed. She stared at the package wrapped so neatly and noticed, for the first time, there was a business card tucked beneath the intersecting twine. "It's hot in here. Maybe I should take that in."

"Good idea. It's probably something really nice, knowing Jonas."

A beat of silence passed between them when they said nothing at all. Aubrey knew Ava was thinking, too, of how devoted Jonas had been to their stepsister. Now what would happen? She could tell by Ava's face that whatever the doctors had told them tonight hadn't been good, which could only mean one thing. Danielle would need her family more than ever.

"I'll see to this." Aubrey broke the silence. "You get Madison inside."

"Ten four." Ava looked on the brink of tears as she dragged her gaze away from the gift, which was clearly some kind of a wall hanging. "Did you get anything to eat?"

Aubrey shook her head. Not that she was hungry.

"I'll heat something up for both of us," Ava decided as she headed inside. The snap of her flip-flops echoed in the empty garage, leaving Aubrey feeling sorely alone.

Okay, call her curious, but she snatched the business card from its secure place beneath the string. The name William Corey was printed in small letters in the lower right-hand corner, in block script. Photographer.

Jonas's friend was *the* William Corey? That's where I've seen him before, Aubrey thought, a little shocked. She'd shelved so many of his books at the bookstore over the years, she should have known him on sight. His picture was plastered on the back jacket of his bestselling collections of inspirational photography. How did Jonas know the famed photographer? And why had someone of William's stature mowed the lawn?

No, that couldn't be right. Could it? Aubrey tucked the card back into place and carefully lifted the wrapped package. It certainly felt like a framed photograph, she thought as she shut the garage door and headed down the hall. It was a good-size picture. Not that Jonas could afford an original, but William Corey *was* Danielle's favorite artist. She had a book of his in the house.

Aubrey took care with the package and leaned it against the wall in Danielle's bedroom. There was a small wooden bookcase in the corner with a collection of devotionals and inspirational books.

There, on the bottom shelf, Aubrey found what she was looking for. A hardback book with William Corey's name on the spine. She tugged it from its snug place and turned the volume over. A man's image with jet-black hair and dark eyes stared up at her.

Yep, it was the same high cheekbones and ruggedly handsome look. William Corey.

It was a nice photograph, she thought, but it didn't look like the man she'd met tonight. His features were the same, yes. His look was the same. But the man in the picture seemed at ease, with a relaxed half smile on his face, standing in a mountain meadow with rugged peaks in the background. He was vital and alive and full of heart. Not at all the man who'd stood in the garage, looking lost in the shadows.

"Aunt Aubrey?" Tyler came up to stand beside her. "I'm lonesome. Will you come watch TV with me?"

"Sure thing, pumpkin." Aubrey put the book back on the shelf, but she couldn't put away her thoughts of William Corey as easily.

She took her nephew's small, trusting hand and let him lead her down the hall.

In the stillness of his mountain retreat, William was comforted by the echoing scuff of his slippered footsteps. He was back in his space, where he was safe from life and the way it made memories tug at the sorrow in his heart.

Hours had passed since he'd driven away from Jonas's house. He'd slapped a sandwich together and called it dinner, then hopped on the Internet to scan through the online version of the local paper. He found a small article saying only that Trooper Jonas Lowell had been shot at a routine traffic stop and was in critical care. Nothing more. He'd tried the hospital, but they weren't releasing any information.

Maybe tomorrow, he'd try harder to see what he could find out and if there was anything he could do to help. After what Jonas had done for him, it was the least he could do.

Troubled, William watched the sun turn bold crimson in the hazy dusk and told himself he didn't long for his camera. He had no desire to capture the light of the sun and the haze of descending twilight. Really. Or, that's what he told himself as the long-dead desire grew razor sharp.

It was that woman Aubrey's fault, he decided as he bent to turn on the lamp at the bedside table. There had been something about her, probably just the trick of the light, that made the dead place inside him come to life. For a moment, he wished for the things that would never be for him again—like innocence and trust and hope.

It had been a long time since he'd prayed. His knees felt stiff as he knelt beside the bed, resting his forearms on the soft, cool percale of the turned-back sheets. The shadowed darkness in the room seemed to deepen and grow; the low-watt bulb in the table lamp wasn't strong enough to keep it at bay.

Maybe it was the shadows within him that seemed so dark. He thought of Jonas's little boy and the promise made. William might have given up believing in nearly everything, but he was not the kind of man who went back on his word, especially to a child. So, he bowed his head and, while no words rose up prayerfully from his forgotten soul, he did find the words that mattered.

"Help Jonas to recover, for his family's sake. Please."

It felt as if he were talking to no one. He was certain he was alone in the room, that God wasn't leaning down to listen to his prayers. That only made the darkness bleaker and the iron-hard place inside his soul harder.

William climbed from his knees, sank onto the mattress and buried his face in his hands. Unable to make sense of the broken pieces his life had become, he lay in the dark, alone.

# Chapter Three

In the antiseptic scent of the hospital's early-morning waiting room, Aubrey searched her father's face for signs of the latest news on Jonas's condition. Even in the harsh fluorescent lighting, John McKaslin looked suntanned and robust for a man in his sixties, but there was no smile in his violet-blue eyes.

"Dani's in with him. There's no good news." Heavy sadness weighed down his voice. "You've lost weight, pumpkin. You look tired."

"It's nothing." And that was the truth. Doing what she could for her family wasn't a hardship, it was a privilege. What was a little sleep lost compared to that? "I stayed to help Ava with the kids, and Madison had a rough night."

"I'm so glad to be here to help out. I'll take over tonight, dear." Dorrie wrapped Aubrey into a caring hug and then held her at arm's length to appraise her. "Your dad's right. You look exhausted. If only we could have come back sooner. John, the girl is exhausted."

Dad shook his head. "We should have come sooner. Spence said Jonas was doing better and to keep on with our cruise."

"He had been." For a little while, it seemed as if Jonas would be fine, and they had all breathed a sigh of relief. Dad and Dorrie had been starting a cruise and Danielle had convinced them to stay on it. That had been before the coma, of course. Aubrey thought the long trek standby from St. Barts and the night at the hospital had to be taking a toll on her parents. "I'll stay here, if you two want to head home."

"All right, then. I'll get some shut-eye." Dad leaned to kiss Aubrey's cheek. "You call if there are any changes, you hear?"

"Yes, sir." It was good to have her parents back in town. She'd missed them both so much since they'd moved to Scottsdale. "You're okay to drive? You must have been up most of the night."

"I got a few *z's* in, don't you worry about me." Dad gave his wife a kiss. "Are you coming? By the look of you, I'd say you've made up your mind to stay."

"Dani needs me, no matter how tired I am."

"You need me to grab you breakfast before I go?"

"No, dear, but how about I walk as far as the cafeteria with you?" Dorrie turned to Aubrey. "I'll be right back. You'll keep an eye on Dani?"

"You know I will."

Aubrey watched her parents amble down the hall, hand in hand, shoulders touching. They had found a good marriage, and it had deepened over the years. Somehow, watching them made her heart ache with loneliness, and what kind of sense did that make?

None. Absolutely none. She ought to be feeling less lonely because her parents were back in town. She wasn't sure what that said about a woman in her late twenties, that she was used to spending so much time with her parents. But she was a homebody. Her family had always been her life and she knew they always would be. It wasn't as if eligible bachelors were exactly knocking down her door. In fact, not one had ever knocked on the door for her.

For Ava. Yes. Absolutely. Her twin had that adorable charisma that made everybody love her. But Aubrey, well, she knew she was a wallflower, the kind of girl men passed by.

It was simply a fact that she'd learned to deal with. Besides, she had so many wonderful blessings in her life, how could she feel right about asking for more?

There was hot water for tea next to the coffeepot in the pleasant little waiting room, so she started in that direction, but something stopped her. A movement out of the corner of her eye. She recognized the gentleman far down the hall at the nurses station. A tall, broad-shouldered, austere-looking man dressed all in black. Why did she know it was William Corey without him having to turn so she could see his face?

Maybe it was the way his wide, capable shoulders were set, as if he were confident he could handle anything. Perhaps it was the shadows that clung to him in the harsh fluorescent light. Whatever the reason, her attention turned to him automatically, as if she had no say at all.

One of the floor nurses pointed their way, and Aubrey watched William turn toward her. Recognition sparked in his dark eyes, and something else—something she couldn't name, but she saw his guard go up. His entire being, body and spirit, stiffened. He marched toward her like a soldier facing a firing squad.

He didn't seem comfortable. He didn't look happy to see her again.

"I was going to give you a call later this morning," she explained. "You didn't need to come down."

"I wanted to." He jammed his hands into his jeans pockets. "They wouldn't give me any information because I wasn't family, but I wanted to talk to Jonas's wife, when she has a minute."

No welcoming greetings. No small talk. He

wasn't the most extroverted man. Maybe that's why she automatically liked him. She was introverted, too. "I'm not sure when that will be."

"I don't mind waiting." William shielded his heart with all his strength. He wasn't going to let himself remember being in the same place in another hospital. In another time. He knew coming here wouldn't be easy, but the antiseptic smell was more powerful a reminder than he'd anticipated. So were the echoing halls magnifying every movement and the sad shuffle of relatives waiting for news.

Enough, he told himself. He had to wipe his mind clean and not let a single thought in. That seemed to take all of his effort, and Aubrey was looking at him as if she wasn't too fond of him.

He wasn't coming across well and he knew it, but this was the best he could do. He couldn't be the only one in this hospital with bad memories. Surely he could handle this better. He had to try harder, that was all.

"I don't know if anyone thanked you," Aubrey was saying.

It was hard for him to focus. The past welled up no matter his best efforts to blot it out. He felt as if he were traveling down an ever-narrowing tunnel and the light at the end of it was blinding him.

"That was really nice of you to mow the lawn."

"Nice?" The sincerity in her violet-blue gaze startled him. He wasn't being nice. He was doing what needed to be done. It was so little to do when he owed Jonas so much. "No. It took all of twenty minutes, I think. No big deal."

"It was, believe me, and bless you for it. We're simply swamped trying to keep everything together for Danielle's sake and the kids."

That only brought back the memory of her holding the small child, awash in light. He might not have been able to capture that extraordinary image with his camera, but apparently he had with his mind. "Danielle. Is there a chance I can see her?"

"She's in with Jonas and he's failing and she doesn't want to—"

He held up one hand, the emptiness inside

his soul splintering like fragile glass. "I'll wait until she has time."

"It might be a long wait."

"I don't mind." He nodded once as if the matter was settled and strode to the first chair he came to in the waiting area. He folded his big frame into it and pulled a paperback book out of his back jeans pocket.

Aubrey watched him flip the book open to a marked page, tucked the book marker at the end of the book and bow his head to read.

Okay, so call her curious and a little protective of Danielle. Her feet seemed to take over, and on autopilot she wound up beside his chair. "Would you like something hot to drink while I'm up?"

"No."

He didn't look up from his book. Not the most talkative of fellows. Aubrey wasn't at all sure she should like this guy, but there was something about him sitting there all alone, his entire body tense, and he didn't look comfortable being here. Somehow the overhead light seemed to glance off him, leaving him lost in the shadows.

Her hand trembled as she reached for the hot water carafe on the heating plate. Why did this man unsteady her? He had a powerful presence and his gaze was sharp enough to cut stone. That ought to be enough, but it wasn't the whole truth. Just as it wasn't only curiosity that had her watching him out of the corner of her eye as she dunked the tea bag up and down in her little foam cup of steaming water.

The volunteer at the desk looked up from the newspaper she was reading, glanced in William Corey's direction and gave Aubrey a knowing kind of smile as if to say, he is a handsome one.

Aubrey *had* to admit that she'd already noticed he was extremely handsome. It was a purely objective observation, of course.

He lifted his focus from his book and studied her through the curve of his long dark lashes. Microseconds stretched out into an uncomfortable tension as his eyes locked with hers. She couldn't tell if he was annoyed or angered, then the left corner of his mouth quirked up into a hint of a grin.

Who knew the man could actually smile?

"What?"

That was sort of an invitation to talk, right? Aubrey dropped two sugar cubes into her cup and headed toward him. "I was wondering how you know Danielle and Jonas."

"I only know Jonas."

"Then why do you want to see Danielle?"

"It's personal."

That's all he had to say. Aubrey stared at the man. He'd gone back to his reading. "I see you're a very forthcoming type. And talkative."

"I can be."

"Talkative? I don't believe that." Did she detect another hint of a grin?

He shrugged one big shoulder. "I'm not here to talk to you."

The corner of his mouth quirked into a definite, one-sided grin, not an amused one, but enough so that it softened the granite features of his face and hinted at a man with a good-humored nature behind the hard stone.

"I owe Jonas a favor, that's why I'm here." His eyes darkened with a terrible sadness.

Sadness she could feel.

He went on. "I want to know what I can do for Danielle. How I can help. Make a difference in their lives." He paused. "The way Jonas had once done for me."

"Jonas helped a lot of people in the line of duty."

"I imagine." He gave a curt nod, as if it were all he could manage. He swallowed hard, and his sorrow was a palpable thing drawing her closer. "I'm not handling this well. It's the hospital. I've spent a lot of time in them."

"In this one?"

"Yes."

She slipped into the chair in the row next to him, leaving an empty seat between them. "Your story didn't end well, did it? I'm sorry."

He didn't know why he was telling her this. What had happened to his resolve to keep this buried? "Four years, five months and twenty three days ago, no, twenty four days ago, my wife died in this hospital. One moment we were riding bikes on the shoulder of a country road, and the next, she was bleeding to death in my arms...."

He could feel the woman's silence like a touch, her gaze on his face, her sympathy as soft as dawn's light. The title on the front of the book he held began to blur. "Jonas answered the 911 call. He was going off duty, but he came to help. The paramedics were right behind him, but I'll never forget what he did. He drove to the hospital and he sat with me while my wife was in surgery. I had no other family. No one else."

That was all he could say. But there was more that Jonas had done, things that had made all the difference. A difference William could not face, much less put into ordinary words. He hung his head, willing the pain down and forcing his vision to clear.

Her hand settled on his arm, her touch light and comforting. He couldn't explain why a sense of peace cut through the well of pain gathering deep within him. Or why she made the agony of an endless sorrow ebb away like low tide on a shore. He only knew how dangerous it was to open up to anyone, to let anyone in, and he jerked his arm away.

"Uh, there's Danielle now," Aubrey said

in a startled voice, hopping to her feet, acting as if he hadn't embarrassed her.

He was too overwhelmed to do anything more than close his book and try to find the will to stand, to greet Jonas's wife with a voice that wouldn't betray his own inner turmoil. He closed off everything else from his mind—even the bit of peace Aubrey had brought to him.

It was just about the saddest thing she'd heard. Aubrey ached for the man as she watched him amble down the hallway toward the elevators. Now that she knew what had happened to him and the loss he'd suffered, she could see that he was walking around broken down to the quick of his soul.

"I can't believe this." Danielle sank into the nearest chair in the waiting room and stared at the business card she held in her hand. "I'm too tired to think."

She looked beyond exhausted, Aubrey thought as she eased into the chair beside her stepsister. Coincidentally, she discovered she had a perfect view of the elevator bank where William was waiting, head bowed, staring at the floor.

He'd jerked away from her. She'd meant to comfort him, and he pulled away as if she were hurting him more. She was embarrassed, yes, but it was nothing compared to the hurt she felt on his behalf.

"That man was William Corey. The photographer." Danielle stared at the card. "I didn't even know Jonas knew him. Wait, maybe I did. My brain is a total fog."

"Did he tell you about the gift?"

"Oh, you mean he wanted to contribute to Jonas's medical fund, except there isn't one." Danielle rubbed her hands over her face, so weary. "I told him about the funds we're accepting for charity in his name. Oh, and I mentioned the auction fund-raiser thing you and Ava are coordinating with our church."

Should she tell her about the anniversary gift? Aubrey wasn't sure at this point that Danielle looked strong enough to take one more blow.

"Mr. Corey was interested in writing a check to Jonas's medical fund, but I told him I wasn't able to think about that much right now." Danielle shrugged. She seemed frayed at the edges, at wit's end, as if her heart had stopped beating. "I've got just about all I can cope with."

Aubrey put her arm around her stepsister. "Did you get some sleep?"

"I'll be fine. I—" Danielle shoved the business card in Aubrey's direction. "I told him you or Ava would be in touch about that donation. It was nice of him, don't you think?"

"I do. And don't worry, I'll take care of it." Aubrey took the card, wrapping her hand around her sister's. She willed all the sympathy she had into a prayer.

It was hard to know what exactly to pray for. For Jonas to miraculously recover? For Danielle's marriage and family to be whole and happy, as before? To turn back time so that Jonas would not have been shot? Some things not even God could change. The past was one of those things.

*Please, Father, make this come out all right.*

But she didn't see how. All she could see

was her sister's tenuous act of holding things together, and the remembrance of William Corey's sadness. She could still picture the steel-straight line of his spine and the inherent sorrow that made him seem so distant and impersonal. But his story clung to her like skin.

How sad is this? she thought, wanting to push it all away like an empty plate. If only she could get this ordeal out of all of their lives. She hated dealing with this constant sorrow and sadness. She liked to look at the positive side of life. She hated the heartbreak and woe that had permeated their family and stolen Jonas from his wife and children.

"Are you all right?" Danielle asked in concern; Danielle who always thought of others even when her world was unraveling at the seams.

"Don't worry about me. I'm just overwhelmed." Aubrey shrugged. "You know me. I hate that things like this ever happen. I would want there to be no hurt and loss in the world. Just goodness and sunshine for everyone."

"Sounds like a good deal to me. If only that were true." Tears brimmed in her dark blue eyes. "What I'd give if we could make that true, but life is a mixed bag of blessings. Some days it's more than I want to face, but that doesn't change the fact that I have to."

A faint bell dinged at the end of the hallway, echoing against the long empty corridor. The light above one of the elevators came on and William Corey moved toward it.

Sympathy tugged at her heart. William looked deeply alone. She watched him wait while a few passengers in the elevator disembarked—Dorrie was among them. She carried a drink carrier and a covered plate, tapping quickly in their direction. But it was the man, lost in shadows, who kept Aubrey's attention as he entered the elevator and disappeared from her sight.

The impression he'd made on her heart remained.

William listened to the echo of his step in the hospital's chapel and wondered why he was here. It was as if he had followed his feet. He couldn't remember making the conscious decision. The chapel had been noted on the main-floor directory and he'd followed the arrows without thought. Now that he was here, he didn't know what he could possibly do. There was no prayer on earth that could comfort him.

Candles flickered in the front of the nondenominational sanctuary, candles that had been lit in hope and prayer. The stillness of the simple place felt as if it still held the memory of decades of deepest prayers whispered in sorrow. Maybe his were still here, earthbound and unheard, from that dark, desperate night long ago.

*I shouldn't have come here.*

He'd thought he was doing the right thing, but now he wasn't so sure. The online article about Jonas's shooting was sparse, and he'd come thinking there was some difference he could make. Sure, Aubrey had told him enough of Jonas's current medical situation to prepare him, but hearing it was another reality entirely. Seeing the look of it on Jonas's wife's face was too bleak a reminder. William knew that look too well, the appearance of exhaustion and desperation. Of what it took to put life on hold to stay at a loved one's side. There wasn't enough sleep, not enough hope, not enough love, no matter how hard you tried, to will that loved one well.

The day's blazing sunshine spilled through two arched stained-glass windows, and the colorful spill of light might be a sign to some who sought comfort in this solemn place. But that comfort and hope had been elusive for him. William's hand felt empty, as empty as his soul, and coming here had been a mistake. He'd been unable to make any sense of life, or reason behind it. It wasn't what he wanted to believe. It was simply all he was left with.

The scent of flowers placed on the altar became cloying, a scent-related memory of when he'd knelt here, praying for mercy to save his wife.

It hadn't happened.

He turned his back to the altar and the cross on the wall, feeling devoid of faith, like a pitcher empty of water, but the pad of approaching footsteps made him hesitate. It was as if the light slanting in thick, nebulous rays through the stained glass brightened when she stepped through the threshold and into the sanctuary.

Aubrey. She recognized him, and their gazes locked. With the way she was haloed by the jeweled light, a hopeful man might think this was a sign that heaven was listening after all.

## Chapter Four

"William." Aubrey blinked but couldn't quite believe her eyes. The man seemed darker somehow even as he stood in the light. "What are you doing here?"

Okay, duh, obvious. Was there any question why she was twenty-seven and single and doomed to stay that way? Her conversation and social skills *could* be better. She took a quiet step forward, careful not to disturb the reverence of the sanctuary.

He didn't answer or acknowledge her obvious question.

"I guess we had the same thing in mind. Prayer," she added when he continued to look at her without saying a thing. "I didn't mean to intrude. I can come back later—"

"No." His baritone boomed like summer thunder. "Don't go. I was just leaving."

"Okay." She remembered how he'd jerked back from her touch in the waiting room. Maybe he was on his way out; maybe he was trying to avoid her.

Way to go, Aubrey. This is where being her twin would come in handy. If she could clone her sister's personality, she'd know exactly what to say to this man who looked slightly panicked and out of his comfort zone.

She moved aside to give him plenty of room to escape. "I always turn to prayer, too, when I feel lost."

He held out his hands, palms up, in a helpless gesture. "I didn't pray. Couldn't."

She noticed his gaze slide lower. She put her hand where he would be looking, at her throat, and felt the small gold cross their maternal grandmother had given her. Gran was a deeply religious woman, and that had always given Aubrey courage. "Danielle gave me your card. My sister and I are trying to handle all the donations that are coming in. Jonas is fortunate to have extensive insurance after all, so we're designating a few charities to donate to in his name. If you're still interested, then just let me know."

A single nod, that was all. His face was stone hard, but now she knew the reason he ambled past her as if he didn't have a heart. No, she thought, a man wouldn't who'd buried his wife.

"I'll get back to you about donations, then." At least she thought that's what his nod had meant. "This had to be pretty important to you for you to come here in person."

He hesitated in the doorway. Turned. He didn't look at her but above her head at the windows radiating light. "It was. I owe Jonas a great debt. Whatever else I may have lost, I still believe in the Golden Rule. In doing right by others."

He left in silence, without a goodbye. Even the pad of his black-soled shoes hardly made a noise, as if he were more shadow than man. Aubrey knew it was just the artistic part of her, thinking of him that way.

In the sanctuary filled with God's light, she knelt and said a prayer for him first.

Whatever reason God had brought William into their lives, and into her path, she hoped she could do the right thing by him. But as to what that could be, she was clueless. She left that up to the angels as she bowed her head and began to work her way down her prayer list.

"I don't know if I'm coming or going."

Aubrey looked up from shelving new inventory at her parents' Christian bookstore to see her twin dashing down the main aisle toward her. "Ava, you're twenty-three minutes late. Again."

"I know it. My bad!" Breathless, she skidded to a stop beside the book cart, dressed in neon-pink from head to toe. "But on the good side, I remembered to bring lunch for you. I did a drive-through at Mr. Paco's Tacos. Is Katherine in yet?"

"No, she's staying with Danielle at the hospital this afternoon so Dorrie can get some sleep. Oh, and Spence got a call from Rebecca."

"Is our wayward stepsister finally on her way home?"

"After a month of missionary work, she says she's looking forward to the creature comforts of indoor plumbing and air-conditioning."

There was a lot they didn't say, but Aubrey knew what Ava was thinking. So many serious issues were hammering hard on their family right now. Spence and Katherine, who both had spoken to their grandmother Whitman on the phone, had concerns about her health. Gran was their mom's mom, who had decided to snowbird in Arizona and wound up staying there for the past few years. So far away, it wasn't as if they could be there to help her out.

Then there was this thing with Jonas, and it had all of them running as fast as they could to help Danielle and the kids get through it.

And then there was Rebecca and her not so nice boyfriend, Chris. It had been a good thing for her to be away in Mexico for a chunk of the summer without phone service. But now she was coming back and Aubrey had real concerns—and so did Ava. She could tell by the dark look.

"What happened to boring?" Ava asked as she snatched an armload of books from the cart. "Remember when our lives were so boring all we did was yawn?"

"If I remember correctly, you were complaining you were bored and kept praying for something exciting to happen."

Ava slid the first book onto a place in the shelf. "I've learned my lesson. I'm never praying for something to break up the doldrums again."

"Be careful what you pray for, huh?" Aubrey teased as she sidled close to her twin and pulled out the book she'd just shelved in the wrong place. "I guess that means this is all your fault."

"What's your fault?" Spence strode toward them, glowering, but he was more bark than bite. "And you're late. Again."

"I know." Ava shrugged as if it was no biggie. "I'm just lucky I could make it at all."

Spence's left eyebrow shot up in a furious arch. "We're truly lucky you graced us with your presence. Aubrey, did she misshelf that book?"

"Not now." Aubrey easily slipped the volume in where it belonged. "Ava's holding down two jobs, and helping out Dani. You could be more flexible."

"I could be, but I'm not going to." He almost said it without a hint of humor.

She wasn't fooled. "Go back to your computer. We've got it covered."

"You'll watch the front?"

"There isn't a single customer in the store. Stop worrying." She often thought that instead of giving her worries up to God, she'd just give them to Spence. He wasn't happy unless he was worrying over something. "Ava brought Mr. Paco's Tacos nachos."

Not amused by the rhyme, Spence jammed his hands into the pockets of his perfectly creased trousers. "No food near the books." He scowled extra hard as if to make up for the ghost of his smile and stormed off.

They watched him go. Aubrey didn't know what to do with their taciturn older brother. She knew Ava didn't, either.

Ava was the first to speak. "Do you know what he needs?"

"Exactly. A girlfriend. But how impossible is that?"

"I've been praying." Ava had an undeniable gift for prayer. "Just like I've been praying for you, too, so brace yourself."

"Ha-ha, very funny. I can't imagine some guy falling for me."

"What kind of talk is that? If I can break my date-only-duds pattern, then you can break this no-dating-ever habit you've got going." Her two-carat engagement diamond chose that moment to sparkle as she shelved a book. "It's all about positive thinking. That, and a lot of prayer. Oh, and the right man coming along at the exact same moment."

"We both know how hard that is to accomplish." Aubrey didn't mind that she didn't have a boyfriend who was so deeply in love he couldn't wait to marry her. Really. Okay, so she did. "Anyway, I love my life the way it is."

"Okay, but that's not going to stop me from praying hard for you." Ava's cell chimed a cheerful tune and she abandoned her shelving to search through her pockets for her phone. She studied the screen and brightened like a star in the heavens. "It's Brice."

Her fiancé. Aubrey pulled the book Ava had misshelved and whispered, "Go into the break room. Go on."

"Thanks. I owe ya. Hello, there, handsome." Ava's smile was 100 percent pure joy as she skipped away, answering the call. Her voice, filled with love and happiness, faded away as she disappeared from sight.

Aubrey hated to admit it, but no amount of Ava's praying was going to help. She was looking thirty in the face and had never been on a date. It wasn't as if she was likely to start now. She was a wallflower and doomed to stay that way. She didn't mind, really. Think of all the blessings she already had in her life. A big loving family. Her left leg, which had healed miraculously enough for her to walk. She had her art and her horse and a good life. She didn't have any business regretting the blessings she didn't have.

And why did her thoughts return to William?

Call her curious. She happened to have a few books to shelve in the next aisle. She'd been in such a hurry, she hadn't taken the time to check out whether they had any of William's photography books in stock. Maybe now was as good a time as any to see, with her lunch break coming up and no one in the store.

She knelt down and found two of William's books. One was a big coffee-table type collection full of rich, colorful photos. She took the other, a smaller collection with text from Scripture, and stacked them on the cart. After all, she'd need something to read while she ate lunch, right?

By the time she'd shelved the first row of books on the cart, Ava had come back into sight, grinning from ear to ear. It was a good thing to see amidst all the sadness and worry in their family.

"Brice is going to do my afternoon deliveries. Whew." Ava was working two jobs to keep her bakery business afloat. "Oh, how about that? You pulled one of William Corey's books."

"I was curious. I mean, I've seen his stuff before." Aubrey shrugged as if it was no big deal. The question was, why did it feel like a big deal? She hardly knew the man. "I just wanted to look again, after meeting him."

"Danielle said he came to the hospital." Ava stopped to flip open the book. "I had no idea. I guess Jonas knew him from some distant tie to the united churches charities. He's a big donor, I guess."

"I'm not surprised." Aubrey thought of the story William had told her, and the truth he'd trusted her with. He'd struck her as a deeply private person, and she didn't feel comfortable saying anything to Ava.

She looked over her twin's shoulder. The first photograph was one of his most collected works, a subtle sunrise scene over the craggy amethyst mountains in Glacier National Park. She recognized the scene because she'd been to Glacier a few times. The lake beneath the mountains glowed as if each rippling wave of water had been painted with rosy, opalescent paint. The photograph seemed to glow with a life— and hope—of its own.

It was hard to reconcile with the man in the chapel. A man who looked as if he'd had all the hope torn out of him. She didn't know why she ached with sympathy for him. Maybe because tragedy had hit her family, too. Maybe. But somehow her sympathy for William felt more powerful than that. As if by sharing his story, she'd seen more of the private man, the tender places within that no one knew.

"Talk about beautiful stuff." Ava turned page after page. "It's a shame he doesn't work anymore. I've heard it's hard to get hold of some of his prints. They're all limited editions or something."

"I didn't know he'd retired." Aubrey thought of the man shadowed and lost. She didn't have to wonder whether he'd put down his camera because of his grief. Of course he had. "I didn't tell Danielle about Jonas's gift, did you?"

"I couldn't bear to, so I talked Katherine into doing it since she'd older, but I guess she tried and broke down in tears, so she hid the gift. Maybe Jonas will get well and be able to give it to her himself. Miracles happen."

Although Ava tried to say it with conviction, Aubrey knew Ava didn't feel it. Neither did she.

Okay, that was about all she could take of all this sadness. Aubrey snapped the book closed. Maybe she wouldn't look at his pictures after all. It would only make her hurt for William, and she needed to do something to counterbalance it. Make a positive in the midst of all this darkness. She had her laptop in the employee closest. Maybe she'd start to answer all the e-mails from the church members about the fund-raiser for Jonas.

Ava snapped her book shut with an echoing thud. "Your lunch is getting cold, hello? Go eat. Put your feet up. Shoo."

"Will you promise to double-check the books you're shelving? Or I'll just have to do it all over again."

"Sure I will. Really."

Aubrey ignored Ava's eye roll and headed toward the back. There was no better fast-food pick-me-up than a chicken burrito and nachos, and boy, did she need one.

William had made his trail ride a long one, stabled Jet, and as he shouldered through the back door to his home, he still couldn't get Aubrey out of his mind. She stayed there the way a half-forgotten dream hung on through the day, with glimpses and images that would not let him forget or push thoughts of her aside. Images of her gentle and luminous beauty had seemed so genuine and, like the pull of his awareness in his heart, remained.

Nothing had been right since he'd first spotted her. He couldn't deny this, not even to himself. He went straight to the fridge and let the cool air wash over him as he debated the choices on his sparse shelves. Finally, he grabbed a bottle of sweetened iced tea, twisted the cap as he closed the fridge door, and took a long pull.

The icy liquid cooled him from the inside out, but did it get rid of that unsettled, sore feeling in his chest? The one that had worsened after he'd told Aubrey about his wife?

Of course not. Not even his strength of will had been able to get rid of that. He wasn't sure what would.

Why had he told her of his most private pain? Maybe he'd felt overwhelmed with Jonas's wife's sorrow and fears, because he knew exactly how she felt. He'd been there, too. Maybe he'd talked about it because the memories had been so near to the surface.

Or, he wondered, was it because he knew it wasn't likely that he'd be seeing her again? She'd been so kind and sincere the story had just tumbled out.

It was too late to change any of it, so he had to stop working it over and over in his heart and in his head. He had to let this go. He headed for the built-in desk in the corner of the huge kitchen. The best course was not to think of it again—or the lovely Aubrey. Then the weight sitting in the chambers of his heart would fade.

It was dark, so he flashed on the lamp on his desk in the corner. The fall of light illuminated a stack of unopened mail, bank statements, fat envelopes from his investment firm, colorful postcards and envelopes signifying junk mail, and his answering machine. There was no blinking light. Pretty typical. He didn't get a lot of calls these days.

Still, he'd hoped for good news from Aubrey.

Aubrey. Just thinking of her made him remember standing in the hospital's chapel and feeling shadows of the past that could not let him go—or that he could not let go of. He didn't know which.

He only wished things could go back to the way they were, where he was numb inside and content enough to be that way.

In the quiet of Danielle's house, with both kids finally asleep, Aubrey found herself on her hands and knees scrubbing the soap ring off the side of the kids' bathtub. Did she know how to spend a Friday night or what? For an exciting follow-up, she planned on scrubbing the toothpaste gunk off the sink.

She heard the click of the front-door key in the lock and the whisper of the door opening.

Her twin, she guessed as she squirted more soap-grime-killer stuff onto the fiberglass. Whatever Madison's bubble bath was made of, it left a stubborn rainbow-colored coating at the water line.

Lucky me, she thought and kept scrubbing. At least she was able to concentrate on the soap ring and *not* William Corey. At least, that's what she was struggling to do when she heard quiet, slow-moving footsteps padding down the hall—definitely not her twin after all. Then who?

She pulled herself off the side of the tub and grimaced. Her muscles were all kinked up from the complicated twisting positions she'd been in so she wasn't exactly moving fast by the time she poked her head out the door.

Danielle's bedroom door was open, light spilling into the hallway.

It was probably Dorrie, come to get a fresh change of clothes for Danielle. She wasn't supposed to be staying over in the room with Jonas, but Dani had vowed a class-five hurricane wasn't going to move her from her husband's side and the nurses didn't have the heart to try.

Aubrey peeled off the rubber gloves only

to find her fingertips were all wrinkly. She hesitated outside the door. "I have clothes in the dryer— Oh, you're not Dorrie."

"No." Danielle stood in the middle of her room like a ghost, she was so weary. "Mom made me come home. She told me to get some sleep."

Okay, call her confused. Why had Danielle left her husband's side? "Dorrie's staying with Jonas?"

Dani nodded vaguely and pushed open her closet door. "I'm going to hop into the shower. H-how are the kids? I've b-been a terrible mother." She pressed her hands to her face, on the verge of tears.

The toll this was taking on Dani wasn't right and it wasn't fair. She laid her hand on Dani's bony shoulder. She'd lost so much weight—too much. "Why don't I run a bath for you? You can sit and relax? I'll bring up some munchies and some of that strawberry soda you love. I hid a can at the back of the refrigerator for an emergency like this one."

"You should go home. I should be taking care of my own kids. I just—oh, I can't do everything and I'm too exhausted to even try."

"Then how about this? Grab your robe, and I'll start the bathwater. Deal?"

"You are a blessing to me, you know that?"

"Impossible. You're the blessing to me." She headed toward the master bath. "Tell me you didn't drive home this tired? You know drowsy driving is just as dangerous as being intoxicated—"

Dani gasped. "What's this? I don't remember putting anything here?"

Oh no. The anniversary gift. Aubrey mentally groaned. She'd forgotten it was hidden in the closet, and that was one more emotional hit Danielle might be too fragile to take. "Don't worry about it. Just grab your robe."

Aubrey popped back into the room, but it was too late. Danielle was already kneeling down to read.

"There's a business card from William Corey. How strange is that? He was at the hospital. I had no idea Jonas had helped him when his wife had been in a coma."

"Spence knows William, too. Spence caught me looking at one of William's books in the break room and had a major meltdown over the expensive book being near a large order of Mr. Paco's nachos."

"Sounds like Spence." Danielle's eyes were already filling. "Is this a picture?"

"William came by to leave that for Jonas. It's an anniversary gift for you."

Tears brimmed Dani's eyes but did not fall. Her jaw dropped as she let the realization settle in. "Jonas planned this. He…"

She said nothing more, but the tears started to fall, soundlessly, one after another rolling down her face. "What was Jonas thinking? This can't be an original. He knows we can't afford something like that."

Aubrey didn't know what the picture was, only that her sister was falling apart. She gently took the robe from the hanger. Her heart was breaking. True love, once found, should not be torn apart like this. "I imagine Jonas would think you were worth every penny that picture cost him."

Dani tugged at the string bow and drew the paper away from the simple black frame. Even in the shadows, the photograph glowed with light.

Staring at the work, her hand to her heart, she thought she'd never seen anything so arresting.

It was no ordinary snapshot. It *lived*. She felt overpowered by the emotional pull. It was a simple shot of a snow-covered evergreen bough, green needles fighting through the mantle of pristine snow. The bough reached upward, like an arm to the sky. A sky where thin, gold and peach rays of sun broke like hope through dismal storm clouds.

The image settled in her heart and in her soul. And it tugged at her spirit like a little reminder of faith.

William Corey, with his artist's eye and poet's soul had been able to capture, for a brief microsecond in time, the divine shining out of the ordinary.

Whatever the man's sorrows, he'd had a gift.

"It's my favorite work." Dani swiped at her eyes. Her fingers came away wet. "It's called *Hebrews 11:1. Now faith is being sure of what we hope for and certain of what we do not see.* One of my favorite passages. And a good reminder."

"It's lovely. Jonas went to a lot of trouble to get this for you."

"I see that. The doctors spoke to me about letting Jonas go. They say he's probably not going to come back. They think he's already gone. That's why I came home. To think over what they said. To figure out what to do. Or at least be prepared if his coma worsens much more, for then there'll be no hope at all." Danielle stared at the photograph, silent for a long time. "But this, it's like a sign."

"What do you mean?"

"I came home too weary, I just am burned-out and worn-out and out of hope." Dani rubbed her eyes again. "This was just the sign of faith I need to go on. When you talk to William Corey, tell him thank you for this. Tell him this has made all the difference."

Aubrey suspected he already knew.

# Chapter Five

The ring of the phone echoed through the dark corners of the great room, shattering the tense stillness of the gathering thunderstorm. William squeezed his eyes shut, but the image of the black storm clouds closing over the sunset's crimson glow remained, along with the desire to capture it on film. A desire he'd thought long gone.

He knew why. Aubrey. For some reason, seeing her had started this. She'd thawed a frozen part of him just enough to feel. Or maybe he'd simply been ready. It had been over four years. They say time heals all things, even, he supposed, a loss so deep.

The phone's insistent ring continued. He

checked the caller ID; it was her. His heart skipped from fear that she was calling with bad news—also an unease that she was calling at all. He'd said too much to her. He'd let the vulnerable truth spill out as if it was nothing, nothing at all. He'd opened himself up too much, and now there was no way to pull back his words. No way to hit Delete, rewind and try playing it differently. He would, if he could. So, why did his hand shoot out and grab the cordless handset?

Because he couldn't stand to sit in the growing darkness any longer. "Hello?"

"William? I'm glad I caught you. This is Aubrey McKaslin."

Yeah, he knew. There was the image of her, graced by the light in the chapel, all purity and sweetness. He'd learned long ago that looks were deceiving, or at least that's what he reminded himself of, so he wouldn't start believing in anyone again. "Hi, Aubrey. How's Jonas doing?"

"He's still in a coma and unresponsive. We're not sure what's going to happen next, though. We're just trying to take it one step at a time."

"That's a nice way of saying they don't expect him to come out of the coma, right?"

"No one wants to actually say that, but, yeah. The chances aren't good."

He squeezed his eyes shut again. He knew what it was like to wait and wonder and pray against all odds.

"William, I have to let you know. Danielle found the photograph you brought over the other night. It made a real difference for her. She said it gave her hope. We have you to thank for that."

"Not me." No one seemed to understand that.

"It was a good thing you did for Jonas. You have no idea what a difference you made."

"It was sitting in a closet, gathering dust."

The warmth in Aubrey's voice told him she wouldn't be fooled. "You did a lot of good for Danielle, and that's making a lot of difference to my family, William. You did that, and I'm so grateful. I wanted you to know."

William watched the black turmoil of the storm clouds crush out the last spears of dying sunlight. He tried to do the same to Aubrey's words. On one level, he'd had a lot of this over the years since he'd been a widower. Whether women meant well or not, too many of them had not been sincere. They'd thought he would be a financially advantageous man to marry.

He knew in his gut that Aubrey meant what she said. Her family mattered to her, the way his once had to him. Maybe that's why she'd seemed to inspire that innate, soul-deep need to pick up a camera again. He was able to see her heart, and it was not so different from his own.

As for the work, what she didn't know was what no one understood. The beauty he found with a lens didn't come from him, but through him. All things good came from God. But it wasn't a discussion he felt up for. He said what was easier.

"If it helped her, I'm glad. How about you? Are you still taking care of your sister's kids?"

"Not as much, now that my dad and stepmom are up from Arizona to help out."

"It must have put a dent in your social life."

Aubrey rolled her eyes. Had she heard him right? "That *is* my social life. I pretty much baby-sit for Danielle most Friday nights anyway, and my big plans for Saturday night are usually with at least one of my sisters. That's it."

"That's it?" He didn't believe it for a minute. "If you're not engaged and you're not seriously dating, then you must have come off a breakup. Right?"

"Where did you get that idea? I'm not the dating type."

"I don't believe that."

"Sure you don't, because nobody is more boring in this entire world than I am. Wait, there might be someone up in, maybe, Alaska, far up in the tundra, if there is tundra in Alaska—what do I know? Whoever that poor person is has probably expired from inactivity. Everyone else on the planet has a more exciting life than me."

"Now, I might have to disagree with you. My life could be more boring than yours."

"Impossible. For example, I'm about to do my favorite thing, and it tends to outbore anyone."

"Let me guess. You were reading a book."

"How did you know?"

"I know about the family bookstore."

Okay, it wasn't a sign or anything, Aubrey thought, but coincidence. She'd always wanted to find a man who understood her love of reading, although clearly William wasn't the answer to that prayer. As if! "I think there's nothing more exciting on earth than reading, but my sisters say that's the real reason I'll never get a date. I think books are the epitome of excitement, but not many guys do."

"Well, I don't know about those other men, but I say it's a good way to spend time. What are you reading?"

"Anthony Trollope. And before you say, who—"

"A popular English author who was a contemporary of Dickens. I'm in the middle of reading *A Tale of Two Cities*. It's my evening entertainment."

"No. You're kidding me."

"Nope. You're not the only one with a love of old and very thick books."

What did she say to that, other than it made him just about perfect?

"How do I tell you that I'm reading my way through the entire Penguin Classics library?" He chuckled. "You're speechless. See? It's true. I make you look like a social butterfly."

"That's a picture." One she couldn't imagine. "Me, a social butterfly? I don't think so. That would be my twin. She's got the gift. She's always been extroverted, so I've always let her—"

"You're a twin?"

"Yep. I'm the oldest by three minutes."

"Are you two identical?"

"Yes and no. We look exactly the same, but our personalities couldn't be more different."

"Then I *might* be talking to your sister right now and think it's you."

"No one has *ever* mistaken me for Ava, unless they didn't know us at all. Trust me, even if we'd wanted to deceive someone like that, as wrong as that would be, no one would believe it."

"Are you two really that different?"

"Night and day. Where Ava got all the social ability, I got all the common sense, which isn't thrilling depending on your point of view."

"Common sense is an admirable quality."

Aubrey rolled her eyes. Notice how he wasn't *interested* in her, as in a romantic thing? That's how men saw her, she'd learned, as the plain and practical one. Sure, it was always good to have basic common sense, but was she the one with an engagement ring on her finger? No. "Easy for you to say. I thought someone who proclaims himself to be boring might understand."

"You see, I like boring. It's not a liability."

"Says the man who spends his Friday evenings reading."

"I have my reasons, but I still don't see why a woman like you is home alone on a weekend night."

An arrow to her heart. Aubrey scanned the apartment's living room. Although she'd tidied up, evidence of Ava was everywhere. A right-footed yellow sneaker—who knew what happened to its mate?—was sitting lonesome and haphazardly beneath the coffee table. A stack of books, listing to the north, had been shoved onto one of the end tables—Ava's books for her premarriage counseling program at the church. Why was she alone tonight? "Because my sister is off with her fiancé having dinner with his parents."

"Fiancé? Then I suppose that means she'll be getting married."

"Yes, in April, and leaving me. I can't believe my luck. I'm finally getting free of her."

William heard the warmth in her words, and the truth behind them. It was tough facing a change, no matter how good it was. "And what about *your* fiancé?"

"My *what?*" There was humor in her words, a lightness that reminded him of the gentle light of a summer's dawn. "I thought we established that I was single—"

"I still can't wrap my mind around it. It can't be true."

"It's true, because I'm dull. I've been passed over by every appropriate man at my church's single's groups."

Passed over? He doubted that. "You don't sound unhappy about that."

"As my sister would say, at our age, most

of the good men have already been snatched up and married off. And who wants the leftovers? They've been leftover for some very good reasons. Besides, I've watched my twin date and that's been enough for me. I don't have to experience them myself to learn from her disasters."

It was her tone that made him smile and brightened him up inside. It had been a long time since he'd enjoyed talking to anyone so much, and he had to know more. "Disasters?"

"There was the guy she dated before she met Brice, her fiancé. On the third date he behaved inappropriately and in her attempt to escape him she accidentally slammed his hand in the car door and broke three fingers. That's only one of more examples of dating gone wrong. I wisely try to stay as far away from those situations as I can."

"Smart move." It hit him like a blow to his chest that he was laughing. He couldn't remember the last time he'd truly laughed. The odd rumble of it vibrated through him and as the first drops of rain drove at the window, the storm didn't feel as ominous.

"I have a fair share of dating gone wrong, as you put it. I stay out of the game."

"Me, too. The entire ballpark. Why try when you know you're going to strike out? My older sister Katherine is getting married next month—if she doesn't postpone the wedding because of Jonas—and she said she was lucky enough to find the real thing, but it took her well over a decade of looking. That idea totally exhausts me. I lack the strength and the will. I'm happier sitting at home watching a storm move in, or reading a book, or watching a movie on the classic movie channel."

Okay, he was going to ignore that she said that. He'd been watching the storm move in. He spent evenings between a classic work of literature or a classic movie. Best not to read anything into the fact that they liked the same things. "So, how did your twin find a fiancé and you didn't?"

"We don't do everything together. Well, we did when we were little and all the way through high school. But every year that we get older, we spend more time apart."

He heard the warmth in her voice, and

although her tone was light and cheerful, he knew what she didn't say. "It's hard to know she's leaving you behind."

"Not behind."

There was love in her voice—the real thing, like a light that never dimmed, like the light he searched for with his camera's lens. Well, before he'd put his work down for good. It was the light that drew him now. He felt himself leaning toward it, toward her, although she was nearly an hour's drive away. Distance vanished as he listened to her words fill with honesty, another rare thing.

"A wonderful blessing has come into my twin's life," she was saying. "I've been praying for Ava's happiness every day since I was old enough to pray. I'm the one who talked her into trusting this guy she's going to marry, and he's good to her. He really loves her, and he gets her. I know I can hand over the job of looking after Ava to him, and believe me, she *needs* looking after."

"Relieved to hand over that job, are you?"

"No kidding."

He wasn't fooled. No, he'd heard a lot of

untruths and falsehoods and full-out lies to know the real thing when he heard it. "You love your sister."

"More than my own life. I have the greatest family. I am deeply blessed. I appreciate them and love them with all my heart. I know a good thing when I see it."

William felt his frozen heart crack a little. The squeeze of pain that followed confused him. He'd kept his heart ice-cold for a reason. Despair had done that all on its own. But now, he felt as if something were struggling to the surface, trapped beneath the ice.

"Here I am, babbling on."

He cleared his throat, but emotion seemed stuck there. "No problem."

"I have another reason for calling. I wanted to make sure you're okay."

It had been a long time since he'd heard that in such a caring way. Her warmth and honesty captivated him and he squeezed his eyes shut, his mind spinning. He remembered how he'd left her in the chapel, how she'd looked like loveliness and hope.

It seemed impossible for him to feel anything again, but real emotion, alive and strong, flared in his chest. Emotions of a deeper nature, beyond the casual simple small talk they'd been sharing. He liked her, but Aubrey McKaslin was getting too close.

That meant only one thing: time to end the call. "I'm fine. Getting along. I'll keep Jonas in my prayers."

"Everyone's prayers are sure helping, I—"

"I've got to go." It wasn't easy to interrupt her. To stop the gentleness of her voice and the bright way she made him feel. Lightning strobed through the roiling black sky in a blinding flash from sky to mountaintop. Thunder crashed as loud as an avalanche rolling downhill, and William didn't know if it was divine help or simple coincidence, but he was grateful for the excuse.

"You shouldn't be talking on the phone. I could hear the thunder from here. William, I'm keeping you in prayer—"

"You take care now."

"You, too." The line went dead the same instant the overhead light winked off. Hail slammed against the windows and the roof overhead. Aubrey set down the phone and went to the living-room window. The storm had drained the last of the light from the evening, and it looked as dark as night outside, except for the brilliant jagged bolts of lightning crackling across the sky. Everything went black, including the other apartments in the building and the entire residential block she could see from her perch.

Maybe she should go in search of a flashlight and some candles. Who knew what Ava may have done with the matches? The chances of finding them had to be next to none. Aubrey felt the edge of the coffee table press against the back of her calves. She'd try the kitchen drawers first, then decide what to eat if the electricity stayed out.

About the time she found a flashlight at the back of the sixth drawer she'd searched, the door flung open with a gust of wind and hammering hail. A faint, familiar shadow filled the entryway and wrestled the door shut.

"Whew!" Ava leaned against the door looking utterly exhausted. "Talk about a storm. I pulled into the parking lot as the lights went out, or I'd probably be snarled up in a long traffic jam somewhere. The street-lights are out, too. Guess what I brought?"

Aubrey squinted at the brown paper bag. Could it be? "Leftovers?"

"Yep! I didn't forget ya, and good thing, too. And guess what? It's still warm. What have you been up to, besides hunting for a flashlight?"

"It would have helped if you made it a habit to put things where they belong."

"I had technical difficulties."

"What a surprise." Aubrey pulled a knife and fork from the silverware drawer and a length of paper towel from the roll. "I never thought I'd ever be lucky enough to marry you off. I can't believe there was a taker for you."

"I know. It just goes to show that true love doesn't find you until you've given up your last shred of hope." Cheerfully, Ava padded into the living room. "I heard from Dad, who'd talked to Katherine who heard from Danielle that Jonas is holding his own. He's not better, but he's not worse. That's a miracle enough for now."

"And something to be very thankful for."

Aubrey slid onto the middle cushion of the couch and stood the flashlight on end on the coffee table. She opened the brown bag Ava had brought her. "Ooh, chicken manicotti. Garlic bread. Onion rings."

"And chocolate fudge brownies are on the bottom." Ava dropped into the reading chair and tilted her head to one side as if she were focusing on something on the shadowed edge of the coffee table.

Right where she'd left the phone, Aubrey realized. And William's card! She reached out to snatch it.

Not fast enough. Ava slapped her hand down on it. "Well, now, what have we here?"

"Nothing. And if it was, it's not your business."

"You have that wrong, Aub. Everything is my business." If Ava grinned any wider, she was going to sprain a jaw muscle. She snatched up the card and kept it protected against her palm, so that it would be impossible for Aubrey to grab. She squinted in the bad light. "William Corey. Imagine that."

"Danielle asked me to keep him informed of Jonas's condition."

"Sure she did." Ava rolled her eyes, reading far too much into that simple, innocent request.

"Don't even go there." Oh, Aubrey knew exactly what her twin was thinking. Her twin with no common sense whatsoever had an imagination that always got her into trouble. "It was totally nothing."

"If I remember right, didn't I say the same thing when I met Brice?"

"Yes, but this really is just business." Not that she'd remembered to tell him much about it. How could she have forgotten? "He wants to make a donation, too."

"Okay sure, but I said it was just business, too, and look at me—engaged to be married to Brice and having had an *almost* successful dinner with his parents."

"No, when you met Brice, you thought he was a yucky man with no morals, propositioning you. Nothing could have been further from the truth."

"Oh, yeah, well, so I was wrong. It worked out."

It was Aubrey's turn to roll her eyes. Ava was wrong all the time, but she wasn't about to argue with her. That would only keep the conversation focused on William, right where it didn't belong. Ava *so* had the wrong idea about poor William. Time to redirect the conversation. "Why was the dinner with Brice's parents *almost* successful? What did you do this time?"

"It's always me, isn't it? Okay, so it was." In good humor, Ava laughed at herself. "Brice's mom had just got this new vase kind of thing. I guess it was worth beaucoup bucks. Do I look like an art expert? No-oo. I decorate cakes and work part-time in a bookstore when there aren't enough bakery orders. What do I know about porcelain or china or whatever antique vases are made out of? So, I said that it was nice, but our sister had one like it she found at a flea market and Brice's mom about had an aneurysm. She choked right there in the dining room on a bite of manicotti. Brice's dad had to give her the Heimlich."

"Sounds like a typical dinner with you."

"It was a disaster. The vase was some

priceless collector thing. How did I know? Although it made Brice and his dad howl with laughter for a good ten minutes. It was even funnier than the time I mistook their conversation on Schubert for the guy who owns the candy store in town. Do I look like a classical music expert?"

"You look like a nut." Aubrey couldn't resist. She loved her sister.

"Don't I know it. I'm waiting for Brice to tear the engagement ring off my finger and run for the hills as fast as he can go, but he says he loves me just the way I am."

"Go figure."

"There is definitely something wrong with that man." Ava sparkled with happiness. "Okay, it didn't work."

"What didn't?"

"Diverting me. I haven't forgotten about this guy." She waved the card in the air for emphasis. "Dorrie said he was so gorgeous, she gave him a nine point five on a scale of ten."

"Why didn't she give him a ten? I would have." The words were out of her mouth before she could stop them. How on earth could she have admitted something so personal? So ridiculous? So not true?

Okay, it was true. But was she prepared to admit that? No. She had to do some back-pedaling and fast. "Not that I was really noticing or anything. But if I were a different sort of girl, one who was looking for a great-looking guy, I might rate him a ten."

"But since you're not the kind of girl who is looking for a great guy, you didn't notice," Ava said reasonably. "I understand perfectly."

"You do?" That didn't sound like her sister. Panic shot through her stomach. "Wait, you aren't planning any matchmaking schemes are you? Remember what happened when you tried to set up Katherine with the copier guy?"

"It didn't work out."

"Didn't work out? The copier at the book-store was broken for three whole weeks because Katherine didn't want to call the repairman to get it fixed. She was avoiding him. I was the one who had to run to the copy shop down the street and get stuff copied. You are a terrible matchmaker. Look at Rebecca."

"That's not a good example. I set them up accidentally."

"You set our little stepsister up with a mean guy."

"I didn't know he was mean. The chef I was dating at the time knew him from a Bible study group. He seemed real nice. How was I to know to he'd be a disaster?"

"Maybe the clue would have been that on date number three you slammed the chef's fingers in the car door when he tried to—you know. Here's a hint. He wasn't a nice guy."

"For the record, I realized that after I set Rebecca and Chris up. And I never meant to break the chef's fingers. It was an accident." Ava rolled her eyes. "What happened to forgiveness? Besides, I wouldn't dream of trying to fix you up. I know that you don't mind having to live alone forever after I get married. I know you like being a single, happening kind of girl."

"That's me." Not. Aubrey rolled her eyes. "I hope the lights come back on. I wanted to start reading my new copy of *Phineas Finn* tonight. And before you say it, I know I'm not going to get a husband sitting home reading an old, thick book, but I like old, thick books and I don't want a husband."

"I don't believe that for a minute. That's dishonest."

It was, technically, because she intended to make it the truth. She would work at it until it was the whole truth, that she didn't mind the feeling of an empty home or looking ahead to a future without a good man to share it with. What were the chances of finding a man who would fall devotedly in love with her? Nil. Men did not fall 100 percent in love with girls like her. It was just a fact of life. And one day, she'd be able to face that fact without it hurting so much.

Not that she wanted to admit that truth, either. Or that her thoughts went automatically to William. "I'm happy with my life. And I love being an auntie. You know I adore Danielle's munchkins and one day, I'll have yours to spoil."

"Scary thought, huh? Can you imagine? That's a disaster waiting to happen." Ava rolled her eyes, but she was beaming joy again. "Well, in good time. I'm not in a hurry. We've got to get Katherine married off first—"

"If she doesn't cancel the wedding because of Jonas's condition. I think she's pretty sure she's going to."

"—then we have to get Jonas well and back on his feet. Then there's my wedding to plan. Then the actual wedding. I want to just enjoy my new life with Brice first before we start a family, so you'll have a couple of years to prepare yourself for the challenge of babysitting my munchkins."

"I can't wait. I'll need that long to gather my strength."

"Oh, here's your book. I'm going to call Brice." Ava pulled the book off the cushion where she was sitting. "I wonder if William likes to read, too?"

"Don't even go there," Aubrey demanded, but she wasn't sure if she was telling that to Ava or to herself.

Too bad, because William was definitely off-limits. And she liked him. Very much. Wasn't that just her luck?

# Chapter Six

She'd been tricked. Duped. Deceived. Days later, behind the wheel of her sensible beige Toyota, Aubrey tried to keep her frustrations at her sister down *and* at the same time keep her eyes peeled for the right driveway, but she'd probably missed it. Nothing surrounded her but wilderness and mountains. The town was nearly an hour away. The directions Ava had scribbled on the back of her bakery's napkins were confusing at best. No surprise there.

What was a surprise? That she'd let her twin talk her into deliveries this afternoon. Now that Dad and Dorrie were in town to help out, she actually had a free afternoon.

She'd planned on working in her studio or updating her Web site or any of the numerous errands that had been put off for too long.

Instead, she'd let Ava, who'd been suddenly overwhelmed with cake orders, talk her into making a few deliveries. She did this all the time for Ava, so why would she suspect that there would be anything out of the ordinary? And there wasn't, until she got to the fifth invoice piled on her front passenger seat and realized that the next delivery was not only way out of town, but it was probably more than an innocent delivery. Ava and Danielle must have concocted this scheme together.

Was that nice, or what? It was a loving thing, that her sisters wanted her to be happy, but they were off the mark. In fact, Ava's harebrained matchmaking schemes were always a sign of sure disaster, so this meant there wasn't the remotest possibility for romance. It didn't matter if she liked William or not, it wasn't as if he were interested in her, right? Besides, she wouldn't allow herself to like him like *that*. End of story.

According to her odometer, she'd already driven the two miles from the end of the maintained county road. Since there wasn't a soul in sight, only trees and an empty gravel road, she pulled to a stop in the narrow lane and went back over the directions. Then she saw it, the unadorned driveway flanked by old-growth cedars, and nosed her sedan down the gravel lane.

But was her mind on her driving? No. It was on William. Would he be glad to see her? She'd tried calling to warn him of her arrival, but there had been no answer. Hopefully, he wouldn't take her showing up with a chocolate cake the wrong way. She steered carefully around the bend in the road. The evergreens were so thick and stretched so high it blocked out all but the smallest dapples of sunlight and most of the sky above. The world and its troubles seemed so far away, and she knew exactly why William had chosen to live here.

The evergreens gave way to a large lush clearing of land. When had she driven off the edge of the earth and into paradise?

Acres of white board fencing, picture-perfect, framed green pasture. Under the shade of a copse of maples sat an upscale stable, made of log and stone. A stable? Did that mean William had horses? She felt her pulse still when she spotted a sleek gray gelding grazing in the green paddock.

William did have horses. That came as a total surprise, but an exciting one. Okay, so there were a lot of horse owners in the world, but it seemed cool that they had this in common, too. It was always great to meet a fellow horseman, right?

She pulled to a stop in a gravelly area beside the three-car garage. Right in front of her, neatly hung from the light pole was a very large No Trespassing sign.

Oops. Well, she might not be invited, but she had legitimate business. She pocketed her keys and grabbed the bag from the front passenger seat. The minute her foot hit the ground, she took a moment to breathe in the crisp, clean mountain air and feel as if she could brush her fingertips across the iridescent blue sky. In the background, mountain peaks speared up with such force and closeness, she felt as if she could reach out and touch those craggy, amethyst peaks. There was nothing but miles of green wilderness to explore.

The ratchet of what sounded like a round being chambered in a rifle echoed in the heavenly stillness. Larks silenced. The wind stilled. Then she heard the telltale metallic clunk of a gate latch falling shut. She turned toward the stable and there he was, William, astride an impressive, midnight-black Thoroughbred. Why did that suddenly make her nervous?

He halted his horse and leaned slightly forward, resting his fists on the saddle's pommel. He looked rugged and masculine in a black T-shirt and jeans. High astride the tall, impressive horse he seemed, somehow, as distant as the shadows. The dappled shade from the tall grove of trees shifted over him, hiding all but the hard, lean lines of his disapproving face. "Seeing you again, Aubrey, is a surprise."

"A good surprise or bad surprise?"

The hint of a smile strained against the line of his mouth. "Depends."

"I brought cake." She lifted the bakery bag as proof.

"Chocolate?"

"Is there any other kind?"

"Nope." At the subtle brilliance of her smile, William felt the protective walls around his heart buckle a tiny bit right when he needed them the most. She was like a refreshing summer morning, radiating innocence and light, and he couldn't pinpoint why. There was simply something innately good about her beyond the image of the golden hair framing her face and ruffling in the mild mountain breeze and more than the sweetness of her smile.

Drawn to her, he pressed Jet into a walk to close the distance between them. "Why did you bring me chocolate cake?"

"It's not from me. I'm just the delivery person." She held the bag so he could read it. There was a smiling cartoon sun on the side of the bag with the bold script, Every Kind of Heaven Bakery. "I'm on a delivery for my sister. Danielle ordered this for you. As a thank-you."

Realization sucker punched him. "What for?"

"Do you really want me to make a list?

There's the lawn mowing and the picture delivery. I guess she also found the book you'd autographed for her. You stopped by the hospital to offer to donate to his medical fund. Your photograph gave her hope when she'd hit rock bottom. Isn't that enough?"

"No." He didn't need anything from anyone—how did he explain that to her? That he might not be happy alone on his mountain, but he wasn't unhappy, either. "I hate to ask how Jonas is doing."

"You know how serious this is."

"My wife's coma continued to degenerate. That's a very distant way to say it, right? Like a line descending on a graph somewhere, as if it isn't about the slow, painful loss of human life. Is that what's happening with Jonas?"

The brightness seemed to fade from her. Aubrey shrugged and concentrated on setting the bag on the top of the low stone fence that separated them. "Actually, he's holding his own. He's responding to deep pain stimulus, or something. Some of his signs have improved. I have no idea what that means or what they are, but Danielle is convinced his vitals change when she's in the room with him. So, maybe between a miracle and her love, it'll make a difference."

In his experience, love hadn't been enough but that didn't mean Jonas would suffer the same fate. "I've been keeping him in prayer."

"I know it helps. Thank you." She gulped in air, as if willing away the sadness. "So, change of subject because it's too hard to deal with."

"I understand. It's why I live all the way out here."

Her gaze met his, full of heart, and he felt the connection zing through his spirit. She did understand. He didn't feel as sorely alone. It was a nice change.

Unaware he'd nudged Jet forward on the lawn, suddenly they were closer to her. The distance between them was no longer yards but less than two feet with only the decorative stone fence between them.

"Hello there." Aubrey lowered her gaze to the gelding. She held out her hand, palm up, for Jet to sniff. "You are one handsome guy."

William's throat tightened, and he dismounted, hardly aware of the horse's low welcoming nicker as he snuffled at Aubrey's slender hand. He didn't need to ask if she liked horses; he figured Aubrey liked everything. William's every sense, every brain cell was captivated by her. Unable to look away, he watched Aubrey smile when Jet offered his nose for a pat.

"How did you know I'm a softy for a good-looking guy like you?"

The tightness in William's throat expanded until it felt as if not even one atom of oxygen could squeeze past. Emotions he couldn't name, and didn't want to if he could, seemed to sit there right behind his Adam's apple. He couldn't talk or breathe. He could only watch as the big black gelding lowered his head and began to lip at Aubrey's jeans pocket. She must have candy.

Jet stomped and huffed, clearly demanding.

"William, your horse is spoiled."

"Guilty."

"You don't sound one bit sorry about that."

"Nope. He's my best buddy."

"I'm sure he's a good one. And a charming guy." Aubrey could feel the weight of William's focus.

The line of his mouth crooked a little higher in the corners. "Jet seems charmed by you."

"I think it's the roll of butterscotch candy." She slipped it out of her pocket and Jet nodded his head as he was agreeing.

"It's his favorite."

"I can tell."

Aubrey noticed the kind twinkle in William's eyes. It was hard to notice anything else as she kept the roll out of the horse's reach and unwrapped the candy. If she kept watching William like this, he was going to leap to the wrong conclusion.

She turned her attention to the beautiful gelding. "I'll have you know that my girl's an Arabian and butterscotch is her favorite, too."

She held the buttery candy on her palm for the gelding to lip up. Jet's mouth was velvety warm and his whiskers tickled her skin as he took the offering and crunched away contentedly.

"An Arabian? For pleasure riding or show?" William asked.

"We used to compete when I was in high school, but now we jump for fun. She's one of my best buds, too." Aubrey knew William understood. "My Annie and I have been through a lot together. This is probably the only time in my life when I've been too busy to see her much."

"You miss her."

"I do. Life can't get much better than when you're galloping with your horse."

"I know that feeling."

Caring snapped in the vicinity of her heart. It would be really easy to like William, to truly like him, in a way that could only be one-sided. Whatever she did, she'd have to be careful, very careful, not to let that happen.

Perhaps she'd better concentrate on the horse. He'd finished his candy and had started to nudge her hand, wanting more.

As if she could say no. She was all marsh-mallow fluff inside, so of course she un-wrapped another candy to feed him. She waited until he was munching away before she offered William the roll. "Would you like one?"

"Sure." He moved a step closer and took a candy from the top of the roll. "You've been riding most of your life?"

"Of course. My gran taught me when I was little." Aubrey took a candy for herself and slipped Jet one more butterscotch before pocketing the roll. "She owns a ranch east of the city. She had a serious love for horses. I got that from her."

"Sounds nice to have shared that with her."

"Her and Grandpop. They used to take all of us kids for wonderful long trail rides. It was some of our best times together as a family. Our mom left when I was seven, and that helped get us through. I was the one who spent even more time at the stables."

"Do you still trail ride?"

"Not with my family anymore. Everything changes, doesn't it? Grandpop passed away a few years ago, and Gran hasn't ridden since. But I'll always have a lot of good memories I wouldn't trade for anything."

William leaned closer, and the empathy on his face showed that he understood. "You know, there's a lot of good backcountry riding around here. Trail riding. Hiking. Canoeing."

Okay, that was too much of a coincidence. "You like canoeing, too?"

"It's one of my very favorite things."

That shouldn't have surprised her, but it did. They had so much in common. She could just picture him paddling through a serene mountain lake, alone, of course. That's how she essentially saw him. She took a step back on the path. "I've intruded on you long enough. Before I go, I've got news on what Danielle's decided to do."

"You mean the medical fund?"

"She doesn't want to take people's money. So many people have offered. It was the first thing the church started to do. But Jonas seems to have great insurance and they aren't hurting at this point. She'd rather donate the money, in Jonas's name, to the widows and orphans fund for the state's lawmen."

"She doesn't believe she's going to lose him."

"If she can, she'll will him well."

He knew what that was like, too. "It's a good cause. I'm still interested in donating. It's the least I can do for Jonas. If there's something else I can do to directly make things easier for Danielle, then you'll tell me?"

"There's more about that than you're telling me, and that's okay. I'm not prying." There was only compassion and concern on her face as she took another step back. "Just ready to listen if you need it. I've put the information for the fund-raisers in the bakery bag."

"I'll take a look at it."

"I'm keeping you and Jet from your ride. I'd better go."

"We're in no hurry." He was at a loss as to why he didn't want to let her go.

She retreated a few more steps into the shadows. "You might want to put the cake in the house first. I'm not sure about the frosting melting or whatever, but it's still, what, in the high nineties?"

"Gotcha. I'll take it in, first." Somehow the words escaped, although the emotion remained lodged tight in his throat, a sharp stubborn tangle he couldn't swallow down or dislodge. He told himself it was because of what he'd told her that day in the hospital, private information he'd kept intentionally buried. That's what this had to be. It was the only thing that made sense. Those had been his truths, his past, times that hurt too much to remember.

He could feel the dark within him, and yet it was not all that he felt. He was aware of the brilliant sunshine, the vibrant summer's heat, the whispering of the green leaves overhead and the warm life of Jet's coat as he nickered after Aubrey. And Aubrey…she made him feel less alone. Every step she took away from him made that lonesomeness return.

She lifted her fingers in a little wave. "Take care, William. Jet, it was nice meeting you, handsome."

The gelding nickered while William stood glued in place, once again unable to speak. Why was it that once again in her presence he longed for his camera? That suddenly he was able to see more of the world and feel his faith?

She moved with elegance and presence; flawlessly except for the limp in her left leg. He'd noticed it before, but he focused on it now. What had happened? He wanted to know more about her. He didn't mean to call out to her. He didn't know he was asking her until he heard his own voice. "Aubrey. Do you want to go riding with me sometime?"

She spun on her heels, one hand lifting to shade her eyes from the glare of the sun as she studied him. For a moment he feared she was going to turn him down, think him a fool for asking.

So, even more impulsively, he added, "Jet wanted me to ask you. He said he'd like the company."

A beaming smile lit up her lovely face. "I'd like that. I'll talk to Annie about it and see what she thinks."

"Then I'll be in touch."

The sunlight seemed to follow her as she turned and picked her way across the rocky border between the mowed grass and the gravel driveway. Even the trees seems to quiet as she passed beneath their boughs, as if they, too, were charmed by her.

She kept her head down as she opened her door and slid behind the wheel. With the sunshine full strength on the windshield, William could see her clearly—every freckle, every curve of her soft petal complexion and her subtle frown of concentration as she buckled herself in and started the engine.

He would never love another woman again. Love had brought him nothing but pain. And it was a moot point anyway, considering that his heart was broken beyond repair. So, why couldn't he turn away from her? She swiped the fringe of golden bangs out her eyes with slender artist's fingers. Light caught on the tiny gold cross at her throat with a quick flash of brilliance that blinded him.

Unmoving, he listened to the crunch of gravel beneath the tires as her vehicle backed up and away. For one brief moment, their eyes met through the driver's-side window. Across the bright sunlight and deepening shadows, William's soul stirred. He watched the road until there was nothing more of her than a glint of sunlight reflecting on the vehicle's rear window. Then only a plume of dust. Then nothing.

Nothing at all.

# Chapter Seven

*Jet wanted me to ask you. He said he'd like the company.* William's words stayed on her mind through the rest of the afternoon and into the evening, even when she was supposed to be concentrating on her Bible study class. Or rather, the lessons of her Bible study class, since it was now over.

Her sister was in the desk across the aisle from her, jamming books into her book bag. "Great class. Hey, so we haven't had time to talk yet today. How did the delivery go?"

"Fine. Just like all the others." She could see her sister coming from a mile away. She gathered up her Bible study materials and slid them neatly into her tote. What she should be doing was not thinking about William, right? Ava wasn't helping. "Will you need help with deliveries tomorrow?"

As if she hadn't heard the question, Ava kept right on talking as she hopped to her feet and wrestled her enormous tote onto her shoulder. "Was he glad to see you? Did you get a chance to talk with him? Did he like my cake?"

"I don't know if he did, since I delivered the cake and left."

"Ooh! You're avoiding telling me stuff on purpose. I know it."

Aubrey settled her book bag's strap on her shoulder. The last thing she wanted to do was encourage this behavior. "You left the keys on the desk, Av."

"I did?" Completely unaware, Ava pivoted in the aisle, spotted her keys, scooped them up and led the way to the classroom door.

Aubrey fell in beside her and they trailed the small crowd filing into the hall. It was fairly crowded for a July evening, and other classes were getting out, too. The hallway echoed with so much commotion. Was it her imagination or did it seem louder tonight than other nights? Louder because of the absolute stillness and peace she'd found on William's mountain.

There she went again. Wasn't she trying to *stop* thinking about the man?

Ava turned to her, eyes full of mischief. "Okay, I need the scoop."

Uh-oh. It was a twin thing. She could tell exactly what her sister was thinking, and there was no way she wanted to talk about William. She wanted to *avoid* discussing William, and the reasons were ones she didn't want to examine too closely. So she went on the offensive. "I hear Spence scared away another prospective girlfriend."

"Sorry, but like that's gonna work. I am the master of distraction. I was trying to get to the bottom of this William thing."

As if she needed help thinking of William. "There is no William thing. Honestly."

"Yes, but you want there to be."

How was she going to deny that? "Have I said anything? No. Not one word. You're reading too much into this."

"Okay, you might not have said anything, but it's there at the back of your mind. Admit it."

"I'll do no such thing. You have romance on the brain."

"I know. It comes from being deliriously happy. You should try it."

"I think I'll skip, thanks." Really, a woman didn't need a wedding ring to be happy. Wasn't her life perfectly fine the way it was?

Yes. So that wasn't the reason she kept thinking about William and his offer to ride together. He had looked good astride his midnight-black horse. Powerful. Essentially masculine. As if hewn of rock, like the mountains that had dominated the horizon behind him. Tender feelings rose through her, but they were *only* protective feelings. She thought of all she knew about William, of his losses and his remoteness. She wasn't interested in him; she wasn't the kind of girl who went around knowingly making mistakes. And how big of a mistake would it be to let herself care deeply for a man who wasn't interested in her? It'd be huge. Enormous. Catastrophic.

"Change of subject," she told Ava, and meant it. There was only one thing that was going to help her put aside every thought of William. Every sigh of admiration. Every ounce of sympathy. "I'm in the mood for chocolate. Want to stop by the ice creamery per usual and pig out on sundaes?"

"Have I ever said no to that?" Ava boldly led the way along the crowded hall, her mammoth bag weighing down her left shoulder. "Hey, I'm kinda tight right now. How about you buy the sundaes, and I'll get 'em next week?"

"Deal."

Poor Ava. Aubrey kept behind her in the hallway, because no one was better than plowing a path through a crowd than her twin. She wondered how on earth she could help her sister more. Business wasn't exactly beating down her bakery shop's front door, but in time Aubrey knew that would change. Jonas was at the forefront of her family's energy, and that's why the bakery had been operating on limited hours. She opened her mouth to offer to man the shop on her days off, but something held her back.

William's invitation.

Wasn't she going to stop thinking about him? Frustration rolled through her. Why was William sticking in her mind like glue?

Because he wasn't in her mind, but her heart. It was hard *not* to have sympathy for him. He was a nice man; it was impossible not to like him. But that was all. She wasn't romantically interested in him. Talk about a totally out there idea.

She was just glad to think about trail riding again. It wasn't safe to ride alone in the backcountry, and she'd lost her trail-riding friend years ago when September's job transferred her north to Whitefish. So, the idea of having a buddy to ride with into the wilderness sounded like a wonderful opportunity.

Oops. What was it going to take to stop thinking about him?

"Okay, what's on your mind? I can tell something's going on." Ava led the way out the doorway and into the hot, bright evening. "I've never seen you so spacey."

"It's been a long day." It was called a diversionary tactic, but it was also the truth.

She'd been up early to help Dorrie with the kids, then a shift at the bookstore after which she helped with Ava's deliveries, then Bible study and it wasn't over yet.

A shout rose above the din of conversation surrounding them. "Hey, you two!"

It was Marin, the youth pastor and a family friend, making her way across the parking lot, hurrying to catch up with them. "Look what I have for you. More donations for the auction."

Aubrey could tell by Marin's excitement that it was something good. She crowded close to see the computer-printed sheet Marin was holding. There was an image of a framed work of art—by William Corey. What were the chances?

"Wow." Ava pushed close to see, too. "That's amazing. We have two other originals, you know."

"I know." Marin was nearly hopping in place. "This is phenomenal. One of my kids just brought this to our youth group meeting. He said his family wanted to help, that Jonas had helped them out once. See? Goodness always makes the world a better place. Aubrey, you can upload this onto your Web site, right?"

"Sure." She saw that the e-mail address of the kid and his family were printed on the sheet, so she could contact them for more information. The trick was going to be keeping her no-William-thoughts vow. Especially with the gorgeous photograph of his in hand.

Aubrey folded the page in half and carefully stuck it in her book bag. "Thanks, Marin. I know you've been behind a lot of the fund-raising ideas."

"Danielle can stay in denial, maybe that's better for her, but she's going to need help."

"She says she feels guilty."

"It doesn't change the fact. It's a generous idea to give the proceeds in Jonas's name to the fund. It's also something we're praying hard she won't need herself."

"Us, too." Aubrey had never doubted her church family was a blessing. Now she knew how very much. "I can't believe how big this auction is getting."

"The donations still keep coming in," Marin agreed. "Oh, I was supposed to tell you two something else, too. When I remember, I'll e-mail it to you. Let me know if there's anything else I can do. Anything, okay?"

"Have a good evening, Marin." Aubrey tugged her little notebook from her bag and slid the folded page into it for safekeeping.

"You two have a safe trip home. I'm keeping your family in prayer."

Something they'd heard too many times to count since they'd stepped foot inside the auxiliary hall this evening. And not just this evening, but since the moment the news about Jonas's shooting had broken.

"We are so blessed," she said to her twin when they were alone in the SUV. "Sometimes you never take a look to really see it."

"And sometimes you do." Ava started the engine and, when the warning bell dinged, remembered to buckle her seat belt. "Now, are you going to spill? I have to know what's bothering you."

"It's William. And before you leap to conclusions, it's not for the reasons you think. He's had a hard time of it. Not everyone is as blessed as we are, with family and friends and a community."

"That's true. You know, Spence mentioned to me that he thought William was a good guy."

"Does Spence know everyone?"

"Our brother is apparently cooler than we think he is. Weird, huh?" Ava put the SUV into gear and checked for other cars. "Spence said William is a decent man, high praise from our critical brother. William gives heavily to the united churches charities. Who knew? Anyway, he's handsome and totally a Mr. Wishable and he likes you."

"Right." Aubrey shook her head. Ava. What was she going to do about her sister? Ava was so not in touch with the real world. Her head was always in the clouds. "Trust me, it's not like that, and I wouldn't want it to be. He's not head over heels over me."

"Why not you? You're a cutie."

"You have to say that. I look just like you."

"Yes, but you're not a disaster like I am. That ought to make you a much better catch than I ever was. So, it only stands to reason that you'll find an even more awesome dude to fall in love with you. Why not William?"

"There's something terribly flawed with your reasoning abilities."

"Okay, that's true, but I'm sure about this. Really." She checked the mirror again and eased out of the parking spot.

William. Why did her thoughts zero back in on him? But it was more than simple thoughts, she realized. She cared about him. Really, truly cared. Whatever hardship came her way, she had family around her. Loving, supportive family to cushion her. When hardship came to her family, she had a loving extended family in friends and in the church. But what did William have?

Alone on his mountain, he had no one. No one at all. Her heart ached for him, and ached in a way that it never had before.

William left his riding boots in the mudroom off the back door and wandered through the house to the echoing kitchen. Early-evening shadows crept through the corners of the room, but the bakery box Aubrey had brought him sat square in the center of the island like a bright pink beacon. Earlier, he'd pushed Jet far into the high backcountry where there was no single sign of civilization, where the wilderness was breathtaking so he would have some chance of getting Aubrey out of his mind.

No deal. He'd been unable to do it. Aubrey's wholesomeness had reached right in and taken a hold of him with such force that he could still feel it hours later. Nothing could make it fade.

She was unlike any woman he'd even known. She was true goodness. It was as obvious as the sun in the sky and how easily Jet had trusted her. How easily *he* had trusted her.

Had he made a mistake asking her to ride with him? He didn't know. But he hoped that she was exactly what he needed.

In such a short time, she had changed him. She was like a little drop of goodness falling into his life, and she made him aware of the automaton he'd become. He'd survived by putting one foot in front of the other and just counting the days go by. That's how he'd been living, empty of hope, faith, everything. And he couldn't do it anymore.

He'd never forget the way she'd looked holding Jonas's little girl in that kitchen the first time they met, or in the chapel with the light gracing her. He'd never forget how she'd looked earlier today dappled with sunlight, lovely as a summer's dawn. That's what made him sit down to the computer at the built-in desk in the family room.

It was the hope for hope that made him begin to type—the hope that his life wouldn't always be like this.

It was a rare night home in their apartment and Aubrey was thankful for it. At the kitchen table, she savored the rich chocolate sundae they'd picked up on the way home and checked off things on the daily to-do list. The kids were accounted for—Dad and Dorrie were watching them tonight. Danielle was at the hospital. Jonas was reported to have incrementally improved, another small victory.

All she had left to do was e-mail the donors Marin had given her tonight. She glanced at the time on her computer screen. That would mean she'd have just enough time to squeeze in a few minutes of reading before prayers and bedtime. It had been another long day, but the days were getting a little easier. She was grateful for that.

As she waited for her modem to connect, she caught sight of Ava in the living room, her feet up on the coffee table, chatting away to her fiancé. She looked so happy, and Aubrey was thankful for that, too. Her twin had had a long string of unhappy romances, so she totally deserved the great guy who'd fallen in love with her.

What was it like to be that much in love? Aubrey didn't know. Sure, she loved reading inspirational romances and a good wholesome romantic comedy and those wonderful classics where true love always prevailed, but that wasn't the same as actually experiencing her own happily-ever-after.

Not that she *had* to have one, but it sure seemed nice. She'd watched so many of her friends find it, and now her sisters. But she'd never come close. She'd spent many of her high-school years recovering from a bad riding accident. Through her early twenties, she'd walked first with a walker, then hand crutches and then a cane. She'd sported a serious limp through her midtwenties. While the limp had faded, her shyness had not. Not dating had become such a habit she didn't even know how to go about breaking it.

Still, seeing her sister so happy made a girl start to wonder just a little. Would there ever be that kind of happiness for her?

And no, that was impossible, she ordered herself before her mind could automatically go straight to William. All she had to do was remember how remote he was, how mantled in sadness to know that he wasn't looking for anyone. He'd lost his heart. It wasn't as if that was something you just got over. Ever.

The computer beeped—she had two new mail messages in her in-box. One from Katherine—a quick checklist for next month's wedding shower she wasn't supposed to know about. So much for that secret. Aubrey mentally rolled her eyes.

And the second message was from William. Talk about a surprise. As she clicked to open it, her heart didn't tug. Really.

Aubrey,

Wow. That was the best chocolate cake I've ever tasted. I owe you a big thank-you for going to the trouble of bringing it out all this way. That's dedication to your sisters. Then again, I think your sister's bakery has a new customer for life. I'll stop by her place the next time I'm in town. Anything else you care to recommend?

And yes, I'm still interested in making a donation. Plying me with chocolate was an excellent idea.

William

Aubrey blinked at the screen. Simply thinking of him was all it took for a lonely ache to come into her heart. Her fingers moved to the keyboard and before she'd made the decision to answer, she was already typing.

William,

While plying you with chocolate wasn't the intent, I'm glad you liked the triple chocolate dream cake. Appropriately named, right? Check out the auction's Web site, I'll put the address beneath my signature. By the way, we just got a generous donation tonight from one of our parishioners. It's an original from an inspirational photographer named William Corey. He's amazingly gifted.

How was your trail ride?

Blessings,

Aubrey.

She hit Send and her heart gave a final, resounding thud. She felt as if she were standing on crumbling ground, as if she could see the pebbles and dirt give way beneath her feet right before she fell into the unknown. Not exactly the most comfortable feeling. Not at all, and she didn't know why William affected her like this.

She didn't want him to.

Now that she'd answered William, she might as well answer Katherine. She was just finishing up that message confirming that, yes, they'd remembered to invite everyone to the shower. Katherine didn't want any of her friends to be forgotten, since it was a "surprise," bless her. One day, Aubrey hoped to be as organized and as together as her older sister. She was ready to hit Send when a new note popped into her in-box.

From William. Really, she wasn't affected by him. And that's the way she intended to keep it.

Hi Aubrey,

William here. I just popped onto the Web site. You have a lot of donations. Count me in. (I'm ignoring the comment about my work—it's nice of you.) I was surprised to see items on the site from a certain talented Miss McKaslin. You should have mentioned you were an artist. One more thing we have in common. I can e-mail you the images for your Web site, or drop off the originals. Let me know.

Jet and I had a great ride. We hit the summit of the Lone Tree Mountains. It was a long ride, but worth it. We could see all the way to Yellowstone Park. Not a bad way to spend a summer's afternoon. Have you ridden that far?

What did Annie have to say about Jet's suggestion?
William.


Okay, she was seriously going to ignore that *one more thing we have in common* comment of his. They had an awful lot in common.


William,
No, I've never ridden that far south. Could you really see all the way to Yellowstone? That sounds like a great way to spend an afternoon to me. Did Jet have a good time, too? Or wasn't he very talkative? I haven't had the chance to stop by and ask Annie her opinion yet. I'll have to get back to you on that.


As she was typing away, she heard a distant, very vague sound but kept typing.


But I think she'd be amenable to it. Her best friend, before he moved away, was a Thoroughbred, too—

"Oh, so there is no William thing, huh?"

Ava's words jerked her out of her thoughts and brought her back into the kitchen where she sat, plain old Aubrey. Apparently, Ava had finished her nightly phone conversation with her fiancé and now she didn't have anything better to do.

"You could be doing your share of the housework," she couldn't help suggesting, but Ava merely scoffed.

"Housework? Please. I am not going to be thrown off the trail, now that I know what's going on. You like William, don't you?"

"William's not *interested* in me."

"What kind of answer is that? You're dodging the question."

"I am, but the answer is obvious and you know why. I have this no-dating habit going, and it's a habit I don't want to break."

"That's not right. You're keeping something from me."

Aubrey hung her head. This was the first time she'd had a real secret from her sister. If Ava knew what William had told her in the hospital and if she'd seen the man's pain when he'd tried to pray in the chapel, then she would understand. But William deserved to keep his pain private. "Trust me, he's just interested in helping with the auction. That's all."

"He must really care about the auction." Ava rolled her eyes, as if she didn't believe any of it, and dropped to her knees to read over Aubrey's shoulder.

As if! "Hey, this is private."

"A trail ride, huh? Very interesting. Don't worry. I didn't see a thing."

Aubrey mentally groaned. How was she ever going to convince her sister that she was fine being terminally single? It wasn't optimal, but she could be happy either way.

Of course, that was easy to say since she'd never met William before. Men like him were no everyday, ordinary occurrence.

Ava climbed to her feet. "I'll lay off, but I want you to know how hard I'm praying for your happiness. I can't go and marry Brice and leave you to fend for yourself."

"You are a nut, you know that?" Aubrey shook her head at her sister, bless her. "Do you have an early start time at the bakery tomorrow?"

"Uh, yeah. I have this huge order of Monster Muffins for a customer pick up at seven. I'll try not to make any noise when I get up at four-thirty."

"I'd appreciate that."

"Get back to your e-mail. You don't want to leave William waiting. Good night."

Aubrey watched her twin head down the hall. Deep down, she knew that Ava was right. There was a William thing, but it wasn't what she thought. It was friendship, nothing more. Maybe that's why she felt so comfortable with William. Because she didn't have to worry about all those pressures and insecurities and expectations that came along with dating.

What she had to do now was finish the e-mail before her server got impatient and ate it.

—so I think Annie will say yes. Let me know when Jet would like us to come up. I'll hitch up Annie's trailer and we'll hit the road.

Oh, you can drop off any donation at the bookstore or Ava's shop. Or I can

always send someone out to pick it up.
Let me know what's convenient for you.
I'll keep you in prayer,
Aubrey

She waited till the message was sent and then logged off. Had she ever felt so comfortable with a person of the male persuasion? Only with family. It was telling. It was a relief.

She and William really could be just friends. They had a lot in common. They were both alone. They were both without riding buddies. With him, she didn't feel like plain, average Aubrey, and it was nice. Very nice.

When she said her prayers tonight, she would remember to put William in them, not only as someone to pray for, but as a friend she was thankful for. What could be better than that?

# Chapter Eight

As she pulled into the small strip mall's parking lot and into a shady spot, Aubrey wasn't sure what mood she was in. It had been several days since she'd exchanged e-mails with William and vowed not to think of him, but had it worked? Not as well as she would have liked.

The minute she stepped out of the air-conditioned car, she started to melt. It was another blistering central Montana summer day, and everything was crackly dry. She did her best not to think of how refreshing the green foothills outside of town looked, and the mountains—and William—beyond them.

She hitched her bag higher onto her shoulder, locked the car and started toward the bakery. The newly renovated shop glistened with charm and newness. The long row of front windows were shaded by a cheerful yellow-striped awning and soft white shades that made the storefront look picture-perfect.

The chimes she'd made trilled overhead when she opened the door. The cool whoosh of air-conditioning bathed her hot face and she sighed. The cheerful sun catchers she'd made that hung along the stretch of windows began to dance as she shut the door.

"Hey stranger." Ava was on the other side of the display case already pouring two large glasses of strawberry milk. "I saw ya comin'."

"Bless you." Something cold was exactly what she needed. It was another long day and not over yet. If she stayed busy enough, then it was easier not to wonder why William hadn't gotten back to her about their ride. "How's business today?"

"About the same." Ava nodded toward the seating area where a dozen bistro tables sat without a single customer. Everything was spotless and lovely but sadly empty. "Except for an early rush for the Monster Muffins and Sunshine Scones, it's been like this."

"Okay, so business isn't exactly booming. That doesn't mean that it won't pick up this September. All those college students will be back from summer break, and you're not too far from campus."

"Yeah, I know. I got another wedding cake order, so that part of the business will keep me afloat. Hey, I got all of Katherine's reading group goodies decorated. Want to help me box 'em up?"

"Sure. Did you get her text-message reminder about the final wedding dress fitting?"

"I don't think so. I haven't looked at my phone for a while. I've misplaced it. Jonas is doing a little better, so that means the wedding is still on?"

"Danielle told her not to cancel it, and it's Danielle's call." Aubrey took a long sip of the cold, sweet milk. It hit the spot. She followed her twin into the kitchen. "What's the plan with the munchkins today? Are they with Rebecca today?"

"Last-minute change. Dad came in to get Monster Muffins for him and the kids for breakfast. I guess Rebecca was supposed to take them all day, but she has a date with Chris tonight." Ava donned a little pair of plastic gloves and went back to work at the kitchen's big table. "So that means we have to take them shopping with us. Dad's pretty tired, and Dorrie is staying with Danielle."

"Okay." See? She had enough to keep her busy between her job and her family. She studied the rows and rows of decorated cookies spread out over the worktable. "You've outdone yourself. Katherine is going to love these."

"I hope so. I was bored of the usual, so I thought, why not make cookies shaped like books for the reading group? It's been fun. Tomorrow's your day off from the store. Do you have any plans?"

"Nothing in particular."

"Aren't you going to go riding?"

Not so subtle. Aubrey took another sip of milk and headed to the industrial sink to wash her hands. She dropped her bag on the counter next to the sink. The second she turned on the water, the door chime rang.

"It's probably Rebecca with the munchkins," Ava said on her way through the swinging door.

Rebecca was seeing Chris. Again. It was another worry for the family, but was she thinking about that?

No. She soaped and rinsed, but was she thinking about her niece and nephew? Her imminent shopping trip and what to buy for Katherine's upcoming shower?

No. Her mind returned to William. To wondering how he was doing alone on his mountain.

As she reached for the paper towels to dry her dripping hands, two black boots came into her field of vision. Then long, strong legs encased in worn denim.

*William.* The paper towel slipped from her fingers. She turned toward him, and when their gazes met, everything within her stilled. It was good to see that he was well.

When he spoke, his baritone moved through her as sweetly as a summer wind.

"Don't look so surprised. You said I could come by."

Did she look surprised? Aubrey fumbled with the fallen paper towel and managed to make her fingers work well enough to pick it up off the counter and toss it into the nearby can. Her voice sounded almost normal when she spoke. "It's good to see you again, William."

The hard line of his mouth softened in the corners. "I thought you might say that. Your sister sent me back here to fetch you. She's looking over the stuff I brought. Come see."

"Sure."

So, it was all business. Whew. Aubrey couldn't exactly pin down why that was such a huge relief, but it sure made it easier to act as if everything was totally normal.

She followed all six feet plus of him through the sunny kitchen and into the cheerful dining room. Light slanted through the window and sparkled in the sun catchers, but he was shadow, stalking like a giant panther through the sun's brightness. He jammed his fists on his hips and stopped short of where Ava stood at the display case, examining two large frames side-by-side.

Aubrey saw the closest photograph first. The visual impact hit her like a punch to the soul, dragging the breath from her lungs. There was a golden eaglet, his downy feathers gleaming like gossamers of gold. He was surrounded by a background of dawn's gentle colors. Peach, gold, rose and lavender painted the streaks of clouds. The fragile baby eagle was caught perfectly as he hopped from the rim of his nest and seemingly onto a bed of clouds ready to cradle him. Light shimmered in those clouds like a blessing. She forgot to breathe as she stared at the image in wonder.

William broke the silence. "It's not technically one of my best, but one of my favorites. Maybe because I was rock climbing when I spotted this little guy across the way. I was hanging almost upside down under an outcropping. I nearly dropped my camera trying to get the shot."

"You rock climb?"

"I've been known to do it without falling." His mouth curved upward to show a hint of a dimple.

Sure, and he had probably leaped buildings in a single bound, too.

The second photograph was even more amazing. It was a winter scene of solemn snow and forest, of hillside and frozen stream at first light, when the world was more gray than bright, more sleepy than awake and tinted in a deep lavender glow. The ribbons of clouds had halted in the sky to admire the rising sun.

It took every bit of Aubrey's effort not to admire the photographer standing at her side.

Ava broke the silence. "How do you do this? You make the light glow like you've put glitter on it."

"It's called waiting for the exact moment to take the picture. That, and having a really good filter."

Aubrey wasn't fooled. This was more than craft, it was a calling. A calling he'd turned away from. One that had made him a lot of money, she supposed, since she had no idea what these pictures would go for in a gallery. But it had to be a lot. This donation of William's was substantial. "Are you sure about this?"

"Yeah. It's for Jonas. And maybe there's a miracle waiting for him. I hope he gets well." Sorrow passed across his face, the way a storm fell across the granite face of the mountains.

Aubrey could feel what he didn't say.

William started to walk away. "I can't walk out of here without taking a look at your desserts. That was some chocolate cake you sent to me."

Aubrey's twin dragged her gaze away from the pics. She beamed at him. "Aubrey told me that you liked it. If you're in the mood for chocolate, I baked some fudge brownies this morning that are totally to die for. Interested?"

"How about a half dozen?"

"Super-duper. I'll be right back. It'll probably take me a while, you know, so Aubrey, why don't you keep our favorite customer company?" She gave Aubrey a telling look and hurried out of sight.

So, the twin had the wrong idea about them. He waited until he heard the door to the back swing shut and they were safely alone before he focused his full attention on Aubrey.

She was still staring at his pictures. Sunlight dappled her with a green and blue glow from the stained glass, and she looked amazing. What made her so infinitely lovely to him wasn't only the way she looked. Sure, she had delicate cheekbones and a small sloping nose, and brilliant violet eyes, but he saw more when he looked at her. Something deeper that shone quietly from inside. She made his guard go down and made him relax. She made him understand how alone he'd become.

"William, you've gone beyond anything we could have expected. I'd say thank you, but it's way too small a word for this."

"They were just sitting around gathering dust."

"Oh, sure they were." She rolled her eyes, not one bit fooled.

She seemed to understand, and he didn't feel comfortable saying more. He'd looked behind and into the past too many times lately, and he couldn't stand to keep revealing it. Some things hurt too much, and always would. He knew if anyone could, Aubrey would understand.

He managed to clear most of the emotion from his throat. "It's the least I can do. It's all I can do."

"It matters, believe me. Would you like something cold to drink? We've got milk, soda, juice, iced tea." She circled behind the counter, reaching for glasses as she spoke. "I'd offer you butterscotch candy, but I'm all out."

That almost made him laugh. "Wouldn't mind some tea. If you're out of butterscotch, does that mean you've been riding?"

"*No.* Life has been too intense. I board Annie at an equestrian stable just out of town. It's just easier. I think this is the first time since our mom left—I was seven— that I've missed so many days of riding in a row." She deftly grabbed a pitcher out of the case behind her and headed his way, balancing two plastic tumblers and a pitcher full of iced tea and lemon wedges. "Annie's always taken care of, regardless if I show or not, but she's my bud. We've been together a long time."

"I understand. You miss her if she's not around."

"I do."

It was strange how he already knew the slightly off rhythm cadence of her gait and the whisper of her movements as she set the glasses on the table in front of him and poured—his glass first. As he watched the golden liquid spill in a perfect waterfall from spout to glass, he wanted to believe that he'd come here to deliver his donation and be done with it.

But it wouldn't be the truth.

"You couldn't live in a more perfect place to trail ride." Her voice shone with wistfulness as she filled the second cup.

Wistfulness. Maybe that's what he was feeling, too. His gaze froze on the line her arm and wrist made holding the pitcher in midair. The tiny, delicate gold chain at her wrist was so airy and elegant, it seemed exactly right for her. He studied the perfect contrast that airy strand of gold made shimmering against the slender, feminine curve of her wrist and hand. Light caught on the glass of the pitcher and transformed the scene.

William itched to have his camera, but he

didn't carry a camera with him. He gritted his teeth, frustrated and helpless. He wanted to capture the moment. With the way the slanted sun cut through the catchers, painting separate rays of light in vibrant, royal colors as a backdrop, it made the simple act of a woman pouring a glass of tea ethereal, touched by grace, sheer heavenly innocence.

He forced his attention away, took a sip of the tea and tasted regret.

She set down the pitcher and slipped into the chair across the small table from him. "One day, I want to find my own place out of town so Annie and I can be together. I stayed at one of the rental houses on my gran's property when I was in college, and it was great having Annie so close. She used to poke her head in the windows during the summer. It was fun. And there were a lot of trails to ride."

"A few weeks ago, Jet and I were up in the mountains behind my house and I saw the very fresh tracks of a grizzly bear along a stream. I turned Jet around and put some distance between me and the creek."

"I'm glad you two got away uneaten."

"Me, too." William took another swallow of the sweet tea, unable to stop noticing her. It was his artist's eye, of course. She made a lovely picture. The way she swept at a few escaped strands of her light blond hair was pure grace. Surrounded by sunlight, she looked like goodness itself. The kind of goodness even a man as lost as he was could believe in.

Behind her, the row of sun catchers winked and twinkled. He recognized the whimsical, intricate scenes from Aubrey's Web site. There was a tiny hummingbird hovering above a honeysuckle bloom. A shaft of sunlight through clouds. The first bloom of a single wild rose.

Those scenes—for some unfathomable reason—reminded him of Aubrey, lovely and simple. Honest. Emotions he would not allow himself to name rolled through his chest.

"The mountain meadows are just starting to bloom with wild roses." He said it without thinking. "When's your day off? Jet and I'll show you."

She narrowed her eyes and studied him,

and it was hard to tell what she was really thinking. "I suppose Annie would like that. How long of a ride are we talking about? I have a few hours free tomorrow. Otherwise, we'll have to wait until Friday rolls around."

"This'll take more than a few hours. Jet likes to take his time when we're on the trail. Friday, then, around ten?"

"Sure, but only if Jonas is doing better."

"I understand."

"Tell Jet I'm looking forward to seeing him again. I'll make sure I pick up plenty of butterscotch candy at the store."

"Tell Annie we're looking forward to it, too." He got up. He couldn't help feeling awkward. It was a lot easier blaming all of this on Jet. William didn't want to think about what was really behind the invitation. He wasn't sure he knew.

He pulled his wallet from his back pocket and tossed a twenty on the table. Aubrey was gazing up at him wide-eyed, ready to protest his paying for his drink, but she didn't have a choice. He cleared his throat. "You'll keep me updated on Jonas?"

She nodded, but any answer she may have

been getting ready to say was cut off as her twin popped into the room with a small pink bakery box in hand.

"With our thanks," the other sister said as she slid the box onto the table. "I still can't believe what you're donating to our cause. It's totally super-duper. Jonas will be awed by this when he wakes up, of course."

William could hardly nod in acknowledgment. He heard the women's words, but he wasn't capable of ripping his gaze from Aubrey. While the woman were identical in looks, he saw the difference. The one wearing the apron bubbled like a mountain creek, while Aubrey was· a quiet stream, running slow and deep. She drew him like the stars to the heavens, and, if he was going to reach out to improve his life, there could be no one better to trust.

She didn't appear to be as captivated by him, thank the heavens. Maybe that's why he felt comfortable with her. Calm. At peace. She was getting ready to argue about the twenty, but he stopped her.

"I've got to get back before the storm hits." It was the truth, but a convenient excuse, too. He took the box and headed for the door. "I'll see you and Annie Friday."

"Yes, but—"

"Unless you've changed your mind about riding with us?"

Aubrey couldn't seem to get the right words out. She didn't want him to seriously overpay for the brownies—or to pay at all. "Uh, no, a twenty's too much—"

"Then I'll take one of these, too." He stopped short of the door, where the sun catchers glinted and swayed. He lifted one neatly off its hook.

"I'll see ya around," he said on his way out the door. The bell chimed, and he was gone.

Aubrey blinked. She knew her mouth was still hanging open—out of surprise or disbelief, she wasn't sure which. She could only stare at the sight of William making his way across the sun-bright parking lot. Dressed in black, he was an odd contrast to the lively green of the trees lining the lot. He paused in the shade beside a top-of-the-line charcoal-gray truck. He drew a set of keys from his pocket and opened the door.

There it was, that raw hurt in her heart, not one of sadness or pain, but because she felt too much. No, correct that. *William* made her feel too much.

She was hardly aware of Ava at her side until her twin spoke. "He's definitely wow. A twenty on a scale of ten. A real Mr. Wish Come True."

Yeah, she'd noticed and she was starting to wish a little, too. That was walking on dangerous ground, so she forced down all the quiet new wishes within her heart until they were silent. It was best to be practical.

"Ava, I think you have marriage on the brain. It must come from decorating so many wedding cakes. It's warping your sense of reality." She said it gently, to tease, to hide the more serious things taking root in her heart. Plus, it made her sister laugh.

"Sure. Right. That's me. But I have weddings on the brain because I'm happily engaged. You know how misery loves company?"

Aubrey nodded, watching as William backed his truck out of the spot.

Ava kept right on chattering. "Well, it's

like that but the opposite. Happiness loves company, too, and I want you to be happy."

Me, too. Aubrey felt the power of that wish with all of her soul. William's truck zipped away and turned out of sight. She was a realist, she wasn't the kind of girl who wished on first stars of the night. She had to be real about this, too. She whipped around and started clearing the table. "What time was Rebecca going to drop off the munchkins?"

"Any second. So, how does it feel to have a date with William?"

"Date? I don't think so. He's lonely. I don't have a trail-riding partner. You know September and I used to ride together, but she moved. That's all there is to it."

Aubrey refused to wonder why William had bought one of her sun catchers. She refused to let Ava's hopes divert her from what she knew to be true. "William is alone. He's gone through a lot of hardship all by himself without the blessings of family and friends and the support that we have around us. That's all this is. You're making too much of it. Really. He needs someone to reach out to him."

"Then I'm glad it's you."

Rebecca chose that moment to drive into sight, and Aubrey was grateful for the interruption. She couldn't find the right words to explain what she felt. Before, Ava had always understood, but now...everything was changing from the way it had always been.

As for William, she knew he needed help. She could *feel* it, but she didn't tell her sister that, either.

She said nothing, watching through the windows as Rebecca, tall and slender and very tan, heaved Madison from her car seat and onto her hip. Rebecca settled a heavy diaper bag on her shoulder and closed Danielle's minivan's side door with the remote. Then, checking for traffic, she took Tyler by the hand.

"Rebecca looks good, doesn't she?" Ava asked.

"Time away from Chris was good for her."

"If only it would stay that way."

They said no more. Everyone in the family had tried to help Rebecca see, but it had only driven her away from them. And now, they had a tenuous peace and at least some closeness.

The kids looked better, too. Tyler seemed more like himself as he charged into the shop. His damp hair spiked straight upward, as if he'd been swimming. "Aunt Ava! Aunt Aubrey! I gotta have some pie. Can I? Pleeease?"

Aubrey let her twin handle it. Emotion still seemed wedged in her throat.

"Sure, thing, kiddo, but only a very tiny, itty-bitty piece." It was their personal joke, which meant a huge slice.

"All right!" Tyler's thongs beat the tile floor in a beeline to the display case as Rebecca let the door swing shut behind her.

"I'm totally in need of chocolate. It's the only thing that got me through two hours of public swim." Rebecca looked tired, but she was still smiling—always smiling.

Although they weren't related by blood, they were more alike than not. Aubrey reached to take Madison from Rebecca's arms. "You sit down. I'll take charge of our prettiest girl and wrap you up a few treats to go."

"Thank you so much." Sweet as could be, Rebecca gave Madison a kiss on the cheek and slipped into the closest chair. "Let me hand over the keys to Danielle's minivan. I just need to give Chris a call. He said he'd pick me up."

Over the top of Madison's downy brown hair, Aubrey caught Ava's worried look. See, this was what Aubrey should be focusing on—her family and their troubles and how she could help even more. But what was at the back of her mind and lurking in her heart?

William. Her attention shot to his pictures that were all hope and heart and soul. She doubted that he knew she would not be able to stop thinking about him. At least she knew better than to tread on dangerous ground.

He was a good man, soul deep. Maybe it was admiration she felt. Yes, that's what this was, admiration. And if it was more, then she didn't *have* to think about it. It wasn't as if there was some rule or law saying she had to examine these feelings and impossible wishes, right?

Right. She could simply deny those feelings and wishes. In fact, denial was a traditional coping method in her family. Who was she to buck tradition? She was a realist. She had to stay in control of her feelings.

With Madison on her hip, she went into the kitchen to box a few chocolate cookies for Rebecca.

## Chapter Nine

An entire week had nearly spun by in a blur, but Jonas had improved and so that meant Aubrey was on her way to see William again. She pulled into his driveway with the trailer in tow, and there he was beneath the shade of the trees where they'd talked before, adjusting Jet's cinch. Dust swirled around her as she stopped the SUV and hopped out, coughing, into the quiet summer's morning. In a navy T-shirt and jeans and boots, he looked ready to ride. A Stetson shaded his face.

William straightened and led Jet by the ends of the reins in her direction. He was actually smiling. "I could see you coming a mile away."

It was an exaggeration, but Aubrey knew what he meant. She squinted against the bright yellow paint job that seemed to attract sunlight and amplify it. "This belongs to my sister. It's shockingly bright, isn't it?"

"I suppose your sedan doesn't have a towing bar?"

"Exactly." Okay, this was going to make her look even more sensible and he was bound to notice. "I wanted a new SUV, but they're fairly pricey, and when Katherine bought a new car, she sold me hers at the balance of her loan, which was way below blue book. I couldn't refuse."

"Practical."

"Yeah, that's me." Not exactly a compliment, but if she'd even had a smidgen of a doubt—the tiniest drop of doubt—then this cinched it. William, like every other guy she'd come across, saw her as sensible, practical. And in guy talk that meant dull. Plain. Boring.

Yeah, she knew. Not that this was anything more than friendship, but for once, she'd like to be thought of as classy and together and remarkable, like her older sisters. But maybe that was never going to happen and if that stung a little, she tucked that down, too, right along with all the other unwished hopes gathering in the bin marked "denial." "Since Katherine's fiancé already owns a house, she has this awesome condo she's not going to need anymore. I'm going to take over the payments, I think."

"Sounds good. Probably close to the bookstore?"

"Yeah. And Ava's bakery."

"I noticed. I stopped by the bookstore while I was town last week. Ran into your brother."

"He didn't mention it, then again, he's not much of a talker. I was surprised to find out that you knew him."

"From the united charities. Seems like aeons ago." He came into the full sunlight and he looked good. Healthy. Better than she'd ever seen him. There was something snappy to him. Well, maybe *snappy* wasn't the right word, but he definitely seemed to be thriving. His smile came easier as he unlatched the back gate to the trailer. "Spence is a good guy."

"That's what we keep telling ourselves." There was no point in boring William with the details of her family dynamics. Jet was close enough that he nosed toward her pocket. "Okay, I'm glad to see you, too, handsome, and yes, I brought candy for you, but you have to wait. Annie hates being stuck in her trailer and missing everything."

A muffled whinny from inside the trailer seemed to say that Annie agreed. Aubrey politely excused herself to the gelding and slipped past William and into the stall. A few quick minutes later, Annie was backing down the ramp, trying to get her head up to look around.

"She's obviously a well-mannered lady." William's baritone was pure rumbling admiration. "Unlike Jet, who has no manners. He kicks and squeals and refuses to load."

"Annie and I are well-traveled girls." She kept a tight rein on her energetic mare until Annie had all four hooves on solid ground.

"You would have to be if you two competed."

"Annie and I liked to travel."

"You miss it. I can see it on your face."

"We do, don't we Annie?" The mare nudged her with her velvety nose, so Aubrey gave her ears a scratch. They'd been together for almost fourteen years. If William thought she was so sensible, he might as well know all of it. "We took a bad fall during a competition. Really bad."

"That's why you limp?"

"I'm lucky that I walk at all, and Annie almost didn't survive. She shattered her cannon bone and it didn't look as if she could make it, but she surprised all of us." Aubrey took a rattling breath, grateful, always grateful. "But we're still together and we're both fine now."

"Annie couldn't compete?"

She nodded. "And while I could, eventually, I couldn't do it without her. We're buds."

"I see that."

Aubrey knew that probably made her look even more dull. Who knew how far she could have gone with her riding? But that wasn't the important part. Her idea of success was the life she lived right now, with her close ties to her family and friends, and Annie, who had been a loyal horse friend. Those blessings were worth more to her than all the money in the world.

"I understand." It was all William said, but his words came so warmly, she knew he did.

"It was a long time ago."

"It must have been pretty severe."

"There are worse things."

She avoided William's gaze and the concern she knew warmed the cinnamon flecks in his eyes. She turned around to fetch Annie's gear but William was already pacing up the ramp. If she leaned to her left side, she could just see him in the dim recesses of the trailer's second stall, hefting the Western saddle and blanket from storage.

How had things gotten so personal between them? She gulped hard to keep all the things she shouldn't be feeling down in the denial bin in her heart. William needed a friend, not more. And she needed…well, she was happy with her life. She had to be sensible. To see this for what it was. If she didn't, then she'd only get hurt.

Just look at him. He was all substance and character, and it was as obvious as the ground under her feet. He emerged from the back of the trailer, handily carrying the saddle and blanket. He was helping her without even asking first. Ava was right. He was definitely a Mr. Wishable. But not hers.

His shadow fell across her as he halted at her side.

"She is beautiful," he said of the horse. He waited for her to take the blanket laid over the saddle. "Her confirmation is excellent. She won a lot of blue ribbons, did she?"

"She has her share." Aubrey carefully grasped the light saddle blanket by the hem. She didn't notice at all how her heart sighed, just a little, from being so near to him.

Focus, she told herself. The point is the trail ride, right? She gently laid the soft fleece across Annie's sun-warmed withers, her sorrel shining red in the direct sunshine. "Annie and I made the Olympic equestrian team, but that was before the accident. She would have won. There isn't a better horse anywhere."

"So I see." So much love, William thought. For her horse, for everyone around her, for her life. Maybe that was what drew him so strongly to Aubrey. It wasn't only her goodness, but she was everything missing in his life. Everything missing within him. It had been there once. He could see so clearly how he'd stopped living, stopped loving and stopped giving thanks.

It was a good thing he'd invited her. His chest gripped tightly, as if his entire spirit were in agreement. He needed this—a real friend—more than he'd realized.

As soon as Aubrey had carefully smoothed Annie's lavender blanket, he eased the custom Western saddle onto the mare's back. He liked the care Aubrey took with her horse, her every moment steady and calm, her voice low and warm. When she tightened the cinch, her mare didn't fight the tightening of the belt around her middle. The Arabian simply reached around to try to grab Aubrey's hat by the brim.

When Aubrey laughed, it was the softest, warmest sound. It reached deep inside him and made him feel renewed. Not a bad thing at all, he decided. Since Jet nickered his un-happiness with less attention, he turned his attention to his buddy.

Everything was going to get better now. William could feel it deep to his soul.

Aubrey couldn't catch her breath. Beauty was everywhere she looked, in every direction. Complete, flawless beauty. God's nature was an incredible place from the Rockies' proud, rugged peaks holding up the western sky to the offshoot mountains and foothills lifting far above the valley floor. Tall, peaceful evergreens crowded together, arms raised to the infinite sky. Wildflowers peeked their purple, yellow and red heads out from between fern and moss to face the sun.

And the wildlife. She'd seen a hawk stroking the sky in large gliding circles, wings held seemingly motionless. Smaller birds, larks and finches and even a few jays flitted away from their perches in tree branches.

She'd missed this. In her saddle, Aubrey felt deeply content. The stillness was incredible, the indefinable sense of calm that stretched from the bottom of the valleys to the silent profiles of the mountains. Only the occasional creak of leather or the jangle of a bridle was a reminder that they were in the backcountry. Even the plod of horse hooves on the sun-baked earth seemed a part of the great stillness.

But the best part of the ride? It was William. He was an excellent riding buddy. He led the way along the trail, an old logging road grown nearly over, and set a leisurely, easy pace. He had a sharp eye, too. It was the photographer in him, she supposed. When he spotted fresh cougar tracks, he'd pull up and gesture but didn't break the majestic quiet. His gaze met hers in understanding as she bit her bottom lip to hold in the sigh of awe. An hour into the ride he drew Jet to a halt at the crest of a rise. She reined Annie in beside him and hardly noticed what lay beyond. All she could see was William.

He seemed at peace here. It was in his posture as he twisted a bit in the saddle to look at her, in the straight relaxed line of his shoulders and the easygoing, kind smile that transformed his rugged face. It was an arresting combination that was all substance. Even the shadows were gone from his eyes, as if he'd been able to leave his sorrows behind. She could feel it in the bright air between them.

Definitely wow. It was hard to force her attention to the meadow stretching out before her as quiet and as lulling as a lake. It was one stunning softly pink carpet creeping over the rise of the mountainside and disappearing out of sight. So many roses, there wasn't a single blade of wild grass to break the fragrant, heavenly beauty. She breathed in the sweet wild scent. "Oh, it's like a secret blessing just waiting here to be found."

"I figured you'd like it."

"Like it? I could just sit here forever."

"I thought you'd feel that way." He paused, as if he were going to say something more, something personal, but changed his mind. "I noticed you use a lot of wildflowers in your artwork."

"I do." Okay, she was a little pleased that

he'd taken the time to notice that about her. He was a thoughtful man, and it only made her like him more. "Do you mind if I take a few pictures?"

"We've got nothing but time."

When she smiled, William knew he'd done the right thing in bringing her here, in showing her this tiny piece of paradise. He knew how it was, wanting to capture emotion right along with that creative inspiration. He dismounted when she did. He took Annie's reins so Aubrey could wander along the edges of the meadow without disturbing the beautiful flowers. He watched while she knelt and clicked away on the little digital camera she'd had in her saddle pack. He watched her wander along the field's perimeter, stopping to look, consider and kneel again to snap more images.

Perfect. That's what she was. Complete, modest beauty. Never had he seen so clearly. The graceful way she smoothed a fingertip lightly over a fragile velvet petal. She was sweetness itself. Sunlight played in her windswept hair, and the summery top she wore was the exact shade of the roses.

Feeling flooded him, hurting like light in a dark place that had been left untouched for too long.

"I've got the best idea for my next project." She glowed with happiness as she rimmed the meadow, heading back his way. "I've been wanting to do more rain chimes, with the fall rains a few months away, and this will be perfect."

"Rain chimes? Never heard of them."

"You'll get the first one for the season, how's that?" She must have enjoyed leaving him to wonder as she stowed her camera in the small saddle pack. "They're like wind chimes, but instead of the wind, they catch the rain and chime."

Sun catchers, wind and rain chimes, he could see the way she took the ordinary and made it a little lovelier. They had that in common, the appreciation of what was right in front of them, and it broke down his reserve, the careful space he kept between himself and other people. He felt revealed as the warm mountain breeze swept over him. Aubrey came close, too close, but he didn't move away.

She pulled a new roll of candy from her jeans pocket. Annie tried to grab it and Jet whinnied a demand, but she only laughed softly as she tore off the wrapper cap. "You two will have to wait. William, you're first."

As William took the first disk of butterscotch, Jet nosed him in the shoulder. The gelding's impatience made Aubrey laugh again, so he gave Jet the piece of candy. The gelding crunched away, causing Annie to lift her lips back from her teeth in protest.

"You're next, you." Kind, always kind, Aubrey slid a butterscotch onto her palm. The mare lipped it up fast, apparently territorial over what she considered to be her roll of candy.

He could see how it was between the woman and her horse. Close friends. They'd been together through a lot. "How long ago was the accident?" he found himself asking without thought of intention. He just wanted to know more.

"I was sixteen, so, what's that, eleven years ago."

"Most horses don't survive a fall like that."

She stroked Annie's sun-warmed cheek. "We had a top-notch vet and a team of specialists, and God was gracious. Annie got through it."

"Pretty well, by the looks of it."

"We rehabilitated together. It was a long haul, but we made it. We have some of our best blessings in our family. My stepmom was—is—amazing. She made sure both of us were okay." Aubrey could sense there was something William wanted to say or ask, and the furrow across his forehead seemed to confirm it. She pulled two small bottles of tea from her pack and handed him one. "My family has weathered a lot of storms together. Our mom took off one day and never came back. Dorrie had a bout of cancer. Katherine had a very hard time. Annie and I had our accident. And now this with Jonas. Up until now, we've come out all right, maybe because we're all together. When something bad happens, and all turns out right in the end, it's not the same as, say, what you've gone through."

William visibly swallowed, as if he were wrestling with his emotions.

"Were you alone?" she asked.

He winced, as if he'd taken a painful blow and turned away to lay his hand on Jet's neck. Aubrey felt her stomach fall. Maybe she shouldn't have asked. Maybe he wasn't ready to talk. Maybe he never would be.

Then he spoke. "Yes, I was alone. My wife was the only close family I had left. My parents had already passed. They'd been told they could never have children and for one reason or another, adoption didn't work out for them. I came as quite a surprise rather late in their life. Mom said she went to three doctors before she believed the diagnosis of pregnancy. They were in their late fifties when I graduated high school. In their sixties when I married. I still miss them."

Aubrey waited while William paused, feeling the stillness of the mountains become more solemn and the caring for him grow stronger. She didn't only hear the love for his parents in his voice, she could feel it in the air between them, in the silence, and in her own heart. He was, beyond a doubt, a big-hearted man. Sympathy filled her, and she waited, wanting to reach out and not knowing if she should.

He gathered the knotted ends of Jet's reins from where they'd fallen in the grass. "In the end, it was just me watching Kylie waste away in a coma. Knowing there was a little bit less of her with every day that passed until she was gone. The accident happened around the time we'd been talking about having kids. So, we never had the chance. When I buried Kylie, there was no one close to me. That's why I owe Jonas so much. I was too numb to deal with anything, and he helped me with the funeral and all the arrangements. On his own time. That was beyond the call of duty, and I never forgot what he did."

She heard what he didn't say. There was no one close to help him through his grief. No one near to help ease that unquenchable loneliness and drowning grief. "What about friends? The church?"

He shook his head, as if he did not have the heart to say more.

"I am sorry." She could feel his pain as tangible as the earth at her feet.

"Home was Chicago. We were on vacation. I'd spent time here before, but I was always working. We were bike riding along some of the country roads that parallel Lewis and Clark's trail when an elderly driver lost control and hit her. I was knocked into the ditch and barely bruised, but Kylie, she—" Pain broke in his voice and he fell silent. The saddle creaked slightly as he mounted up. "I couldn't leave her grave to go back home, so I stayed here in Montana."

Alone. Aubrey had never hurt for anyone as much as she did for William. "But you had friends. Extended family. People you could trust who cared?"

"Yes, and no. I pulled away." Settled in his saddle, he spun Jet away from her, keeping his back to her.

But he couldn't hide a thing. She could feel the broken pieces of his heart in the deepest core of her being. A pain too deep to measure. A loss too huge to ever overcome.

"I pulled away," he said with a hollow voice, "because it seemed like everywhere I turned there were people trying to take advantage."

"Like reporters? I don't remember anything in the papers."

"It didn't merit a lot of attention at the time. In Illinois it did. I'd gone back home at first to make the arrangements, to have the funeral there, but I was inundated. Overwhelmed. The reporters were part of it, but to this day it still surprises me that there were some women approaching me every time I turned around. Women who basically thought the grieving widower might be an advantage to them. They were gold diggers, and I couldn't believe their nerve. I'd lost everything; and then I lost my illusions about people, too."

"*Some* people," she corrected him.

When he didn't answer, she mounted up, too, not at all sure if she should. They were surrounded by such beauty, by God's grace in every flower and tree and rock. This did not feel like the right place for such darkness and sadness. "If only there was something I could do for you."

At first, William didn't move. Not a flinch, not a tensing of a single muscle, not even a breath. Maybe he hadn't heard her, she thought. Then he spoke.

"You already have." He pressed Jet into a quick walk and headed east, as if into the rising sun.

"There's one more thing I want to show you." William broke the long stillness that had settled between them. It wasn't easy. What he wanted to do was to retreat back into his silence and withdraw. To put distance between them and keep it there. He hadn't revealed so much of himself to anyone since he'd lost his wife. He'd been without reason or purpose or heart ever since, but something had changed standing at the edge of the field of roses.

Maybe it was being able to see the world so clearly again, or maybe he was starting to live again. Something that had been so hard to do, because real love was everything. He did not think he could find meaning in a single breath otherwise. And now Aubrey's friendship had made him begin to see and feel with his heart again. He hadn't even realized how long he'd been standing as if in utter dark, and the world, in contrast, was so blindingly bright.

Aubrey moved alongside him, quiet and serene on her gleaming red horse. He'd probably been along this trail a hundred times, but he'd never seen the lake shine so brightly, as if a hand had reached down from heaven and polished it until it gleamed. The deep greens of the trees, the softer greens of the grass, the gray granite of the rocks and the lavender faces of the mountains were all so vibrant it hurt his eyes—and his heart— to see.

"It doesn't look real." Aubrey's whispered words were an awed hush. "It looks like someone laid down a mile-long sheet of perfectly hammered pewter."

"It's the light. In an hour's time, the sun will be higher in the sky and it will turn blue like an ordinary lake. It's the mountain's reflection that makes it look gray."

She nodded as if she understood. "This is where you canoe."

"Yes." He let silence settle between them again, and he wanted to press Jet into a walk. He felt safer with distance, but distance wasn't what he really wanted. Old habits died hard. He'd developed a scarred psychological skin and had worn it for so long, keeping people away was his natural MO these days. It took conscious effort to take a deep breath, let it out and stay where he was. His heart beat thick and hollow. "Would you like to go canoeing with me sometime? Maybe something a little more exciting than a placid lake?"

She let the silence settle, too, and he couldn't help but think they were more alike than different, the two of them.

When she answered, she sounded as if she understood what he was offering. Not just a chance to go out in a boat on the water, but friendship. Friendship and nothing more. "I haven't been canoeing in so long I've probably forgot how to row."

He chuckled. "Then that's a yes?"

"Annie, what do you think?" It was hard to tell exactly what Annie was thinking, but Aubrey's smile said it all. "It would be wonderful."

Wonderful? Yep, that was the word. William wasn't ready to end their ride just yet. "There's a forest service road just down the way. I'll take you back on it, if you want.

It takes longer, but it's the scenic route. Might come across some deer, maybe some elk. We'll have to see."

"Then it's a good thing I have my camera with me."

That's what he wished he had, his camera with him to capture the morning. No, not the morning, he realized, but her. Light filtered through the evergreens to burnish her, like liquid gold, highlighting her light blond hair platinum, softening her lovely features until she was too good, too sweet to be real and not a dream. It was like seeing her for the first time, all of her spirit's beauty that was so rare.

"Hand over your camera." He reached out, and her eyes smiled at him as she laid the small camera onto his palm. He could read her face, so honest. She was unaware of his feelings and of what she meant to him. She probably had assumed he wanted a few stills before the light changed and the lake became ordinary, for she turned to watch the water a moment longer. And, so revealed, he snapped a single shot of her.

"Hey!" She scowled at him, but only

Aubrey could make a scowl look cute. "No fair. I am *so* not photogenic. You have to erase it."

"If that's going to be your attitude, I'll have to pocket this."

"William. You can't keep my camera."

"Watch me." Sure enough, he slid it into his shirt pocket and wheeled Jet toward the shore, once again leaving her to follow.

She knew he wasn't truly going to keep her camera, but why had he taken a picture of her? Her hair was windblown, her face was probably a little pink from the sun, and her riding hat's wide brim always made her cheeks look chubby.

Fab. Just what she wanted recorded for posterity.

"Are you coming?" he said at the lake's shore, twisting in his saddle to look up at her. His eyes were sparkling; his grin was relaxed and genuine. He looked like a whole new man, a man without shadows as he rode into the full light. "If you want your camera back, you'll have to come with me."

He needed her friendship, this man who had lost everyone he'd loved. She could feel it as surely as if he'd said the words. Okay, it was nice to be needed. She felt her heart fill and her spirit brighten. She braced her feet in the stirrups, ready for the steep, downhill ride to the shore, where William was waiting.

For her.

## Chapter Ten

Talk about a fabulous ride. The effects stayed with Aubrey through the rest of the late afternoon and into the supper hour. Nothing could dim her joy. She'd spent the afternoon running errands for Danielle and now she nosed her car through Danielle's subdivision.

It was hard to keep her thoughts from going over the morning spent with William. After all, she'd had a lovely time. She felt bright from the inside out. Wasn't it always a wonderful feeling to find a real friendship? She signaled and turned onto Dani's street. She liked William. She enjoyed spending time with him, but her family was not going to understand that. She knew the parameters of the relationship, but they were all going to leap to conclusions. She'd just have to set them straight, right?

Right. She spotted the dozen cars parked in front of Danielle's house. She managed to wedge the SUV into a spot curbside and, after grabbing the shopping bag with her contribution to tonight's supper, she faced the blistering heat of the July evening. Still one hundred degrees in the shade, and she felt every degree as she made her way up the cement walkway to the front door.

Why was she remembering how temperate it had been on the mountainside with William? Surely it was the sweet, soft, wild wind she was wishing for because it had felt so pleasant. Not scorching and sticky and oven hot. Which was the reason she was wishing she was still up in the mountains. It wasn't as if there could be another reason, right?

Right.

The front door swung open and Ava bopped down the porch steps with Madison on her hip. "Okay, tell me. I gotta have the scoop. How did the ride with William go?"

Aubrey stopped to give Madison a kiss on the cheek. "Thanks for the use of your SUV. Annie and I had a great time."

"Oh, of course you two did. I'm sure being with William had nothing to do with it."

"He has this gorgeous Thoroughbred." Diversion, that was the key to keeping Ava distracted. "How's Dani doing? Was she able to leave Jonas today?"

"She's afraid he's going to wake up any minute and she has to be there when he does."

"Yeah, I get that." There was still a lot of doubt about the extent of Jonas's brain injuries, but it was too scary to think about. "Is Dorrie staying with her?"

"Yep."

Ava said nothing more, but Aubrey knew what she meant. While it was miraculous enough that Jonas was becoming more and more responsive, there were still so many worries.

Unaware, Madison leaned trustingly

against Ava's shoulder and held up her chubby arms. "Ay! Pap-op."

Aubrey melted, as she always did for her little niece. "Hello, pretty girl."

Madison's pure blue eyes sparkled. "Ah! Nah-no-gup."

"Really? Well, me, too." She gave a kiss to Madison's baby-soft cheek and received a wet smack in return. "Good girl."

The thud of little-boy feet thumped in their direction. Tyler raced into sight, his fireman hat askew. "Aunt Aubrey! You gotta come see! Uncle Spence 'n' me, we're fightin' fires!"

"Wow, cool. I can't believe you left Spence all by himself. He needs your help, buddy."

"Yeah, I know!" He raced off again, making siren sounds that echoed in the cathedral ceilings.

Aubrey dumped her purse and bag in the entry closet and stood in the cool draft of the air-conditioning vent. That's what she needed. And, since she was back to thinking about William, it was amazing that the serenity she'd felt on his mountainside was with her still. "Seeing Tyler like that is heartening. He's doing better, too."

"It feels as if life just might go back to normal, right?" Ava led the way into the kitchen, where Katherine was busy at the stove tonging ears of corn from a bubbling kettle.

"Hey, there." Katherine looked up from her work. "And exactly why are you so late?"

Aubrey winced. She could tell by her sister's warm smile, that she already knew the answer. She set the bag on the counter and pulled out two loaves of French bread. "I had to get Annie settled in, and I had a hard time leaving her. I haven't been spending as much time with her."

"I see. The horse. Is that the story you're going to stick to?"

"With all my might."

"Okay, I understand the importance of denial. But for the record, great choice. This is *the* William Corey. Spence sings his praises, so that has to mean he's a great guy. And that's exactly what you deserve, sweetie."

See? She'd known this was coming. She had to set the record straight. "First of all, it was a trail ride, not a date. It was *so* not a date. And Ava, I know that look—"

"What look?"

"That one. It's pure mischief. Don't even go there." Oh, she knew what was coming next. How this was about romance, this was about falling in love with Mr. Perfect, and Ava couldn't be more wrong.

Really. If they knew what *she* knew about William, they would see that very sensibly.

Ava rolled her eyes on the way through the kitchen to the dining room. "I can't believe this. You got to tell me when I was trying not to date Brice, how he was so right for me. And so good for me. And now I don't get to do the same to you?"

"Uh, no-oo. This is not the same thing. I need you both to drop this. It's not like that with William. Really."

"Okay, *sure.*" Ava didn't look convinced as she slipped Madison into her high chair, deftly corralling the little girl into place despite her attempts to escape. "And here I thought it was your one chance to break that no-dating habit you've developed."

"Not all habits are bad or need to be broken. For instance, daily flossing can be a very good habit."

"But chronic nonsocial behavior isn't."

"I'm not nonsocial. I'm just shy, which is something you will never be able to understand." But William did.

Ava rolled her eyes. "Okay, so I'm not shy. You don't have to be, either."

"Sure, I'll just toss this personality away and grow a new one."

"That's the spirit!" Not an ounce of mischief had faded from Ava's face.

Apparently, Aubrey would never be able to convince her twin of the obvious.

"Aubrey." Spence strolled into the room, drenched as if he'd taken a hit from the sprinkler. Little Tyler loved to pretend he was a fireman and play with the garden hose. But being a preschooler, he didn't have the best coordination with the nozzle. "I hear you had a date with William Corey."

"Not a date. How many times do I have to say that?"

"Well, whatever it was, I hope you thanked him for those pictures he donated. I took them over to the gallery and the owner nearly had a coronary. I guess they're worth huge bucks. You should ask him if he wants to help more with the auction. Not with more donations, but to volunteer. He's big on that, and it might be good for him."

Uh-oh. Even Spence? "We're only friends. Just friends. I'm not going to explain it again."

"Oh, sure." Spence didn't look as if he believed her, either. "Still, he might want to help out. Anyway, did you remember to bring your laptop?"

Now there was the Spence she recognized: all work. "Yes."

"Okay, then." He gave her a very appraising look, as if he were trying to figure out this William thing, and stormed off.

"With him it's all work, work, work." Ava shook her head. "I don't think we can have a family get-together without him having a purpose behind it. Tonight it's work-on-the-auction stuff. On Sunday it will be to start taking down Katherine's rose trellises so he can transport them to Jack's house. What are we going to do with him?"

Katherine poured the kettle water into the sink with a steamy whoosh. "I tried fixing him up with a friend from the reading group, but he refused to even consider it. He said she was too flighty."

"He says that about all women." Ava adjusted Madison's high-chair tray and handed her a sippy cup.

"It's just a defense." Aubrey could see her brother so clearly. Sometimes it was better not to get involved beyond a certain point, especially when you knew you would get hurt.

It was better to be smart and practical in life and in love. That, in her opinion, was a good habit to follow. Not even a wonderful trail ride with such a good man was going to change that.

William stared at the image on his computer screen, the image he'd downloaded from the digital card in Aubrey's camera before he'd returned it to her. At the time, she'd made a comment about images of the field of roses and the lake and he'd said nothing. He didn't want to tell her that he wasn't interested in those shots. That wasn't the reason he'd taken the camera from her.

*This* was. He stared at her image on the screen, framed by light, taken in a quiet moment. Her beauty shone from the inside out, and he was thankful he'd caught her with the lens the way he truly saw her. With his heart.

You know what that means, man. He felt fear thud in the chambers within him. In all the years he'd been tucked on this mountain away from civilization, from people and anything that would remind him that he had no life, he'd never been able to do this. To see once again with faith and hope and capture it.

Even if he'd wanted to.

He had Aubrey to thank for that. Her friendship had made a difference in his life. So much so that he still felt the peaceful aftereffect in the evening hours. The sunset spilled through the wide picture windows of his study and hit the royal colors of Aubrey's sun catcher. Light and color glowed like a promise.

He reached for the phone. He couldn't say why. He did notice that the loneliness bothered him, and wasn't that a change?

·The phone rang twice before she answered. "Hello?"

"Aubrey. Bet you're surprised to hear from me so soon."

"Something like that." She sounded happy and bright. "We were just talking about you."

"We?"

·"I'm at Danielle's house with my family. I forwarded my home phone to my cell," she explained over the background noise. "We're updating the auction's Web site. Spence says hi, but I really think he's annoyed with you."

There was humor in her words, and that made him curious. "Why, what did I do?"

"As much as we love that you donated your pictures, do you know how many e-mails this has generated in three days? Two hundred and eleven. Spence has answered thirty-six, so it's going to be a long evening."

Now he hadn't considered that. "I should help."

"As if you haven't done enough? You don't need to volunteer, too."

In the background he heard a man—probably her brother Spence—say, "Tell him yes."

Aubrey kept going as if she were ignoring the comment. "Although you're welcome to volunteer, you shouldn't feel obligated."

"I know. And I'm still offering."

"Really? Well, we'd love to have you."

She eased the lonesomeness within him. He studied her image on his computer screen. "Of course, it's not really a generous offer, now that I think about it. It's after eight and it takes an hour to get to town from my place. You'll probably be done for the night by the time I get there."

"There's always tomorrow."

"That, I can do."

"Great." Aubrey felt bright from the top of her head to the tips of her toes. "We're meeting—ah, where are we meeting after church tomorrow?"

She looked at the expectant faces of her nosy family—bless them—gathering around Danielle's kitchen table to listen in as she talked with William. Why couldn't she remember their plans for tomorrow?

"My condo," Katherine said in that calm way of hers. "Remember?"

That did sound vaguely familiar. Then it hit her. Yikes, she was starting to sound like her twin. This was so not her, forgetting everything. She wasn't behaving like herself. That could *not* be a good sign.

"Ask William if he likes barbecue," Katherine urged.

Ava added her two cents from the kitchen counter. "Tell him I'll make something chocolate if he comes to dinner."

Aubrey felt her cheeks heat. She knew William had to be able to hear them, since no one was bothering to lower their voices.

Spence leaned close. "Invite him to church. Hear that, William? You should come. It's the early service at the Gray Stone Church."

Hayden, Katherine's soon to be stepdaughter, looked up from playing a learning video game with Tyler. "Is that, like, Aubrey's boyfriend?"

She listened to William's warm chuckle.

At least, he thought this was amusing, because she didn't. Embarrassment was creeping across her face. Her nose was turning strawberry-red. Another bad sign. Could it get any worse?

Before it could, she got up and walked away from the table. "I'm sorry about that boyfriend comment, William. My family is getting very carried away. You are invited to come over tomorrow, as a friend of the family, if you still want to meet them. They can be scary, but only in the nicest way, of course."

"How about I look for you at the service and we'll go from there."

"That would be perfect." It meant everything to hear the understanding in his voice.

"What can I bring for dinner?"

As if he needed to do one more thing for her family? "We've got it covered. Just come."

"I guess I'll see you tomorrow, then."

"I guess so. Goodbye, William."

She waited to hang up until she heard the click on his end of the line. When she looked up, she realized that she'd wandered all the way to the back deck, just for a little privacy. There, through the large living-room window, she could see her family watching her and debating among themselves just exactly what kind of friend William was.

This was wholly private, what she felt. Friendship, yes. Admiration, yes. Respect, yes. And anything more than that, she didn't have to acknowledge. Just like she didn't have to acknowledge the brightness shining secretly in her heart.

Determined to keep feet firmly on the ground, Aubrey pocketed her phone and went back inside. There was more computer work waiting and dessert to help serve and kids to get into bed. She would concentrate on that. Not on William.

William set the phone in the cradle. The sun had sunk lower toward the western mountains, and the spill of light through the window came lower, beneath Aubrey's sun catcher so that it no longer glowed and winked. The simple rose in the glasswork made him remember how she'd looked beside him at the edge of the field, and how she'd made him feel.

It had been a long time since he'd really trusted anyone. He'd glossed over the devastation he'd felt after losing Kylie. For so very long, he'd been alone and glad to be. Trusting no one had been easier. Staying away from others, trustworthy or not, had saved him from caring. And from caring, getting involved. Because love hurt too much.

But Aubrey, she was different. Simply talking with her affected him. He could feel the warmth in his heart like the gentle new glow of the first star of the night. Not romantic, no, it wasn't that kind of glow. Deep down he was so hungry for the ties of family and friends that, as scared as he was, he needed this. He needed Aubrey's friendship. She was one woman he could trust with that need.

While she stood in front of Danielle's pantry shelves with a notepad in hand, Aubrey listened to the sounds of Katherine, Jack and Hayden's final goodbyes to Dad and Dorrie at the front door. It had been a good evening with her family, with the excitement of thc growing interest in the Web site's auction items, and the call from William. Danielle was still at the hospital, refusing to leave Jonas, and the strain of it, according to Dorrie, who'd spent all day with her, was starting to take its toll.

She recognized Spence's footsteps behind her in the quiet kitchen. She didn't turn as she scribbled down another item on the list. "I'm almost done."

"No hurry. I'm waiting for Dorrie to pack a new overnight bag for Danielle. I've got some casserole dishes to return to a few of the church ladies, and I'm swinging by the hospital, too." Spence had that tone in his voice. The seriously serious one. "Did I hear Ava right? Did she try to set you and William Corey up by having you deliver a cake to him?"

"The cake was a thank-you from Danielle, and a setup only works if the two people are interested in being set up." She noticed the peanut-butter jar had nothing but a few scrapings in it, and she added that to the list. "Don't worry, Spence. I'm not looking for an engagement ring from William."

"You're a sensible girl, unlike some others I can name in this family." While Spence looked gruff, Aubrey wasn't fooled. Not a bit. Not at all. She couldn't help adoring her big brother who had taken care of them all through tough times and good. He'd always been there, grumbling, sure, but he'd never let one of them down.

He was simply trying to take care of her now as he lowered his voice. "No one knows William real well, but I know this. He gives heavily to the united charities and he's done it for years, and he's never wanted anything in return, not even a mention of it anywhere. Whenever the soup kitchen is running low on funds, all one of us on the board has to do is call him and there's a check when we need it. He's a reliable and upstanding man, and if he's interested in you, maybe you should take down a few of your defenses."

"You know something about defenses, do you?"

That actually made him smile. "Not me."

"I didn't think so." If anyone had impenetrable defenses, it was Spence. She knew why. He'd been hurt the most after their mother left. She schooled her face, kept her emotions steady and all while adding macaroni and cheese to the grocery list. "You don't have to worry about me, okay? I'm just friends with William. We're riding buddies. He's all alone, and I hadn't been riding in the forests since my old riding buddy moved, you know that."

"Sure." Spence nodded as if he saw her clearly. "Just think about what I've said."

She didn't have to. She ripped the list from the pad and handed it to her brother. "The list is arranged by aisle, if you start at the vegetable side of the store."

"That's very practical of you. You're great, Aubrey. Thanks." He walked away, pocketing the list. "Good night."

"'Night." She closed the pantry door and waited a moment in the empty kitchen, letting the emotion settle.

Dorrie padded into sight. "Aubrey, are you all right?"

"I'm good."

"Are you sure, dear? You look terribly sad."

"It's nothing, really. I'm all right. Did you need something?"

"Tyler's asking for you to come read his bedtime story. Would you mind? I know you wanted to get home."

"You know I can't say no to my nephew."

"I thought you might say that." Dorrie's loving smile said it all. She came and gave Aubrey a hug. "I've got the book all set out. Tyler's prayers are said and he's tucked in."

"Then you go enjoy a little unwinding time in front of the television. There's a new series starting on Masterpiece Theatre."

"I might do that. Thanks, dear. Are you sure you're all right?"

"I am."

Dorrie didn't look as though she believed her.

Aubrey felt very plain and practical as she turned out the kitchen light and headed down the hallway. She'd told Dorrie the truth. Everything *was* all right; nothing was hurting but her heart.

## Chapter Eleven

There she was. The instant William found Aubrey in the crowded sanctuary, his uncertainty faded. It was hard taking this step, harder still to stand with his guard down in the resonant church loud with the sounds of rustling movements and conversations as families settled onto the long pews. Hardest of all was to let in just a little hope.

"William." When she looked up to find him at the end of the row, her smile seemed like a confirmation. "Believe it or not we've been saving a spot for you. If I can get Ava to move all her stuff. Ava."

"I'm hurrying." Her twin, beside her, was busily trying to stuff numerous items back into an enormous tote. "I can't find my Bible anywhere."

"It's probably right where you left it last," Aubrey said patiently. "Like on the night-stand at home."

"Oops." Ava sounded as if she wasn't all surprised. Apparently this was a frequent occurrence. "I'll just share with my handsome fiancé."

William recognized Brice Donovan from the many times he'd made donations to the united churches board. After saying hello and shaking hands, he nodded to Spence, who was much farther down the row with the rest of the family.

Aubrey scooted over to make room for him next to her and he settled in awkwardly. Church was a place made for feeling, and letting any emotion move through him had been something he'd fought so hard against for so long. It overwhelmed him now. He held back as hard as he could and still he felt, hurt with the newness of it.

Aubrey's smile made the stinging sharper. Her low alto drew him closer.

"I'm glad you came," she said in that

gentle way of hers. "I sort of thought that it would all be too much, with my family and everything."

Remembering the boyfriend remark he'd overheard should be enough to keep him away, but he could look into Aubrey's violet-blue eyes and see her honesty. She understood. Gratitude moved within him like light through the stained-glass windows, transforming him just enough so that he could stay. Relax. Feel comfortable at her side.

As for her family, he understood. They were close-knit and protective of her. Something he'd once known and lost, so he got exactly how precious it was. "Don't worry. I understand."

When she smiled, his heart did, too.

She leaned closer. "How long has it been since you've been to a service?"

"Years. It hurt too much to go alone. My wife and I—" He shrugged, unable to say more. He didn't have to. It was a comfort to know that he didn't have to say some of the hardest things out loud. She simply understood him.

The music started. Since everyone was standing and reaching for the hymnals, he did the same. Aubrey's soft, perfect alto didn't surprise him, but what did was the sense of closeness he felt to her.

It felt good, not to be so alone anymore. He was glad he'd come. He had a lot to give thanks for.

Poor William looked lost, Aubrey thought as she peered out Katherine's front window. He stood in the condominium complex's parking lot holding a shopping bag in one hand and studying a piece of paper in the other. A laptop case hung by a strap from one strong shoulder.

"You'd best go save him," Katherine said, as she carried the covered bowl of marinating chicken from the kitchen to the back patio door. "I'll take care of setting the table so you don't have to worry about it. Just go help him."

Yeah, her sister *so* had the wrong idea. Aubrey rolled her eyes, wishing she knew what to say that would make them believe her. The truth wasn't working; only time would show them. She headed straight to the front door. She hurried not because her heart took a dive at the first sight of him, but because the units weren't uniform and the directions could be a little confusing.

She hardly noticed the blistering heat radiating off the blacktop as she headed out the door and onto the front step. Did she notice the sweet honeysuckle scenting the air? Or the kiss of sunlight on her skin?

No. There was only William and the way his face lit up when he saw her. The shadows were gone, and a lot of his reserve. Once, she'd thought him as remote as the mountains and now he was her friend.

"Hi, stranger," she called out, shading her eyes with her hand.

"I guess I'm not lost after all. I was just getting ready to call you." As he walked toward her, his smile widened to show real honest dimples.

Not that she should be noticing that or how handsome he looked in his black trousers and matching shirt. Or how self-conscious she felt in her best lavender dress and matching sandals.

He fell in beside her and said nothing.

A huge silence grew between them. Quick, Aubrey, think of something entertaining to say. Something engaging. Funny. She searched her brain, which had gone totally blank. Well, she shouldn't be surprised. She'd never been full of interesting things to say.

William broke the silence, bless him. "This is the place you're going to buy?"

"Yeah. It's like home anyway, since we— I mean, I—spend so much time here. Ava and I are always imposing on Katherine. Well, that was before she got engaged. She had more time on her hands before Jack popped the question, so we helped her fill it. It won't even feel like a real move. I think half of my things are in the guest room."

"Then it sounds like a real sensible purchase."

Yep, that's me, she thought. It was a good thing to be sensible. Really. That wasn't what was bothering her, if she were honest with herself. No. If she were honest, then she would have to admit she'd been holding on to a tiny hope that William might see her differently. That he might see more in her, beyond the plain and the sensible woman, to the real Aubrey McKaslin.

It was best not to think about all that. "Spence and Dad were just getting ready to barbecue. I hope you like chicken."

"I like everything. I've never been a picky eater. Which reminds me." William held up the large bag. "I stopped by the farmer's market and got some fresh corn."

On the cob. Sure enough, the bag was full of green husks of corn, the tassels a perfect light gold. "You get full marks."

"I'm not done yet." He said nothing more, but his dark eyes were warm with a secret. His smile, so relaxed and bright, made him seem like a whole new man. He stepped into the shadowed foyer after her. "I brought my laptop. I figured it might help out with the online stuff."

"Great. After dinner, we plan to have a huge e-mail session. Even more messages have come in since late night, so we should be busy. Oh, and Ava brought dessert. Her triple-chocolate dream pie."

William had a hard time focusing on much of anything aside from Aubrey. She was all he could see. From the soft shine of her golden hair to the sweet way she talked and moved and smiled, she drew him like the stars to the sky. At peace, he followed her into the large gourmet kitchen. "Where do you want me to put the corn?"

"Oh, on the counter is fine. Would you like something cold to drink?" She opened a stainless-steel refrigerator, and the wide door engulfed her as she began rattling off the choices.

All he could see of her was the hem of her lavender dress and her matching shoes. Cute. Perfect. Nice. Not that he was supposed to be noticing.

"Lemonade," he decided, managing to get the word out of his tight throat. Maybe it was the aftereffect of the service that was weighing on him. Once his guard had gone down, it had been slow going back up. He felt too full of feeling—emotion he wanted to ignore instead of analyze—and eagerly took the glass Aubrey had filled and set on the counter. The icy coldness eased some of the ache in his throat, but not the big one dead center in his chest.

"I have something for you." He set the glass aside and opened the laptop case. Inside was the eight-by-ten he'd matted and framed. "I thought you might like this."

"Oh no, it's not of me, is it?" She didn't cut her gaze to the picture but instead her eyes met his. It was impossible to read what the shadows in them meant. Impossible to understand why she looked troubled. "I *knew* I should have stolen my camera back sooner."

"I wouldn't have let you. Aren't you even going to look at it?"

"I hate to look at myself in pictures."

"Sorry. I want you to look at this one." He felt like saying more, something about how beautiful he thought she was, or telling her how amazing she looked today. He wanted her to know he had nothing but respect for her.

The thought of saying any of those things, well, it made him feel uneasy. It would suggest a deeper closeness between them that didn't exist.

Or *if* it did, he couldn't acknowledge it.

Her fingers brushed his as she took the frame from him. Peace filled him, and he didn't want to acknowledge that, either, or the fact that he couldn't take his eyes from her. Still, she had not looked at the image. He had to ask. "What do you think?"

Then she looked. She didn't react right away.

Why did that make him nervous? It wasn't like him to hang on what other people thought, but he *had* to acknowledge that her opinion did matter to him. This photograph meant something to him.

Seconds ticked by and she didn't move. She didn't blink or seem to breathe. She didn't smile to say that she liked it, or frown to say she didn't. Nor did she hand him back the photo. His heart began to beat hollowly. There was no way watching her that he could guess at her feelings. He'd never known anyone else who'd been able to keep thoughts and reactions so private. They had that in common, too.

Finally, he broke the silence. "I thought you'd like a picture of you and Annie."

"You thought right. This is incredible. Annie looks—" She didn't finish. "She looks like the champion she is."

"I got a lucky shot."

If that were true, Aubrey thought, then William had been lucky every time he clicked the shutter. This was no exception. How he'd managed to capture the exact moment when Annie had lifted her head to scent the wind, Aubrey didn't know, but somehow the mare was sheer, frozen motion. The fluid ripple of her red mane, the flowing texture of lean muscle beneath sunwarmed satin, and the gloss of sunlight on her sorrel coat made her shine like a dream against the background of blinding blue sky, polished lake waters and rough-cut amethyst peaks.

As for the image he'd caught of her, she didn't even know what to think. She was mostly suffused with the fall of sunlight falling over her. She would have been washed-out had anyone else taken the picture. But, instead, she looked surrounded by light, as if the sun had deigned to lean low to touch the earth and she happened to be in the way. She'd been watching the lake, her hair spilling down from beneath her hat and rippling in the wind at the same angle as Annie's mane.

She didn't look like herself. Sure, it *was* her, but she wasn't plain or ordinary. The woman on horseback did not seem overly sensible or practical. She looked opalescent, tranquil and self-possessed.

Katherine spoke; Aubrey hadn't even been aware of her coming into the kitchen. "This is amazing, William. It looks just like her."

"I think so." William's baritone rumbled with sincerity.

"That's how you see me?"

When he nodded, her heart fell and didn't stop. How perfect was he?

Don't fall in love with this man, Aubrey. But how did she stop the emotion rolling through her with the power of all her unac-knowledged hopes and most secret dreams? Wishes that went beyond friendship. Dreams of happily-ever-after with this man who could see her.

Was it possible? Not as things stood now. What was she going to do? How was she going to keep these new, uncertain affections private? Was it on her face, and, if she said one single word, would her voice give it away?

Spence saved her. He marched into the

kitchen as if he owned it and placed the marinade bowl into the sink with a *clunk*. "Corn? Great. I'll get this husked. Katherine, you'll boil some water?"

"Sure."

Katherine's moving around and Spence's departure were background because, as hard as she tried, she couldn't seem to make her brain jump out of Neutral. Only one thing was clear. She was in deep jeopardy, and William, he didn't even know he was so dangerous to her.

She propped the frame on the counter, so the rest of her family, who were sure to make their way into the kitchen, could admire William's work.

She wasn't falling in love with him, really. As she headed toward the arched doorway, she tried to convince herself she was in perfect control of her feelings. "C'mon William, I'll show you the backyard. Katherine has done a gorgeous job with it."

William said nothing as he followed her. They walked in companionable silence, neither saying a word.

It was safer that way.

\* \* \*

William had retreated into silence behind the screen of his laptop; it was the most distance he could create between himself and the McKaslin family without actually getting up from the dining-room table and leaving. He wasn't sure what that said about him, that he fought a jagged-edged panic being so near to anyone.

But the truth was, as much as he wanted to get away, he also wanted to stay. He'd had the best time. He hadn't realized how hungry he'd been for an evening just like this one. He liked Aubrey's family. He liked their ties of caring and connection. The shared history. It made him remember his own.

Aubrey sat beside him at the oval table and leaned close to speak low, so only he could hear. "How are you doing? Are you ready to run away from us yet?"

"So far so good." He winked. "You know, now that I have access to your server, I can help out during the week from home."

"That would be wonderful. I want to say that you've done more than enough, but on the other hand, we really need the help."

Wasn't that just his luck?

From across the table, the oldest sister was watching them approvingly. William hoped she wasn't reading more into his presence here than there was, and it made him a tad uncomfortable. He knew it was well intentioned, but love was the last thing he ever would want again. He was glad Aubrey understood, and that was what mattered.

Katherine spoke above the hubbub of the other family members working away behind laptops at the table. "It's a comfort to know that there have been so many people who have wanted to help. People we don't even know, who Jonas has touched in some way through his job or the church. It helps balance out the tragedy. Don't you think?"

Her words, while they weren't directed at him, troubled him. He wasn't sure what to say, because that wasn't his view of life. He wasn't sure what to say.

"That's what everyone says," Spence muttered as he tapped away at his computer. "It's a trite cliché. Nothing makes hardship better. We're just supposed to say that, but it's not true."

The other twin, Ava, made a face. "Yes, we've all heard your tough view of existence. Life is hard and then you die. Do you know what you need, Spence?"

"Is there any way to stop you from telling me?"

"Nope, sorry." Ava sparkled with mischief, apparently living to torment her older brother. "You are a terrible pessimist. You need to turn that around and start thinking optimistically."

Spence frowned, but there was a hint of humor in his voice. "I don't believe in optimism. William, you're a sensible sort. Maybe you can explain life to my little sister who has been hunting and pecking at her keyboard for the last hour, unlike some of us who've actually been *working*."

William still didn't know what to say.

"Hey!" Ava defended herself. "I don't know how to type. Really. Oops. I think I did something wrong. Aubrey, how do you get something back you've sent?"

"This is a disaster. Let me see what you've done." As always, Aubrey sounded patient and amused.

Why was she so revealed to him? Why could he see so much of who she was? He'd never been able to see anyone so clearly. The depth of love for her family, her commitment, her values, her spirit. When he looked at her, it was as if he was back at the lakeside, holding a camera in his hands and seeing through the lens, seeing all of her, seeing what mattered.

That panicked him. A whole lot. What he should be doing was packing up. It was getting late and dark would be falling. He had a long drive home and chores waiting. So, why wasn't he eager to head out the door?

Everyone at the table broke out in laughter; he'd missed what had been said, but he didn't miss the fact that these people stuck together, regardless of tough times. On the wall behind Aubrey was a collection of framed photos, some in collage mats, some in single frames, and all of family. They'd welcomed him in their midst today, and he was glad. It made the lonesomeness inside him fade.

The sound of the front door opening

silenced everyone. Aubrey's twin popped out of her chair, engagement ring gleaming. "It's Brice back with the ice cream. I'll better go help him, he was going to pick up—"

That was as far as she got. A golden blur streaked through the archway and into the room. Ava dropped to her knees and the streak became a golden retriever who gave her a few swipes of his tongue and barked in greeting.

"—his dog, Rex!" Ava finished, and the rest of the women abandoned their work to pet the dog.

"Too bad he can't type," Spence muttered from behind his computer screen.

Yeah, William knew what he meant. It was hard to open up at all. He found it much easier to stay tough and stone-cold.

This was his only defense.

He closed up his laptop and reached for the case he'd left behind him, against the wall. He wasn't keeping track of Aubrey, really, he wasn't, but he couldn't come up with any rationalization to explain why he kept her in his sight. He noticed the moment she became aware of his packing up. She didn't turn to look at him but tilted her head slightly to listen to the zip of the computer case. Tension slipped into the slender line of her shoulders.

The oldest sister spoke first. "William, you can't go yet. Not without a second round of dessert."

"I've got livestock to feed."

"That's right. You and Aubrey are both horse lovers. I suppose you aren't boarding your horse?"

"No, I have enough land. I don't mind doing the stable work."

Katherine nodded slow and sure, as if she approved of him completely now.

Yeah, he knew what she was thinking. Aubrey was right. Her family was kind, but they didn't understand. They wanted the best for her, of course. They looked at him and saw a single, Christian man who happened to be well-off. Wouldn't that be a good situation for their beloved Aubrey? On the surface, he looked marriageable. But underneath, not so much. Underneath there were the broken pieces of his heart that had no pulse, no life.

Aubrey came to him. "Did you want a piece of pie to go?"

"No, I'm too stuffed from dinner. That was some barbecue. Thank you, all."

"C'mon," Aubrey said in that quiet way of hers that drew him so. "I'll walk you out."

"Thanks for the help, William," Spence called out. "I'll e-mail you."

"Good."

Everyone called out wishes for a safe drive, a good night and thanks, as if he'd done something extraordinary. No, coming here had been terribly selfish, he realized as he stopped on the way out of the room to pat the retriever who was grinning so widely he drooled.

The truth was, William had come here tonight to save himself. He didn't realize it until he stepped out into the evening. Twilight hovered like a promise at the edges of the eastern horizon, and the air and sky were mellow. He was finally alone with Aubrey.

She fell into stride beside him. "I can't believe you made it through the entire day with my family."

"Why not? They're great people. It's a special blessing, to have the gift of such a family."

"I'm grateful for them every day."

The blacktop was still radiating heat, and the air was hot, but there was the scent of cooling in the wind that rustled the trees lining the parking lot. It was only the hush that came with the gathering twilight, but to Aubrey it felt like more.

William had fit right in. He'd helped Spence and Dad and Jack dismantle some of Katherine's gorgeous trellises, and when that work was done, he'd tried to help with the dishes, although Katherine had refused to allow such a thing. He'd bantered right along with the family through the e-mail-answering session. It seemed as if William belonged with them.

Even now, her steps and his steps tapped in synchrony and their gaits fell into rhythm while they wandered along the sidewalk toward the guest parking area.

William's pace slowed as his truck loomed closer. "We didn't get a chance to talk about that canoe trip I've promised you. I'll even pack a picnic. Not just bologna sandwiches, but a real nice meal. How about this week sometime?"

"Sure," she managed to say as if it wasn't a big deal. But it was. Huge. Enormous.

Don't think about how perfect it feels to be standing with him like this, making plans, just hanging out. Because that would be acknowledging the worst possible thing that could happen. It would make her admit, even to herself, how much she had fallen for this good man when she had no business doing so.

William fished his keys out of his pocket. "Then it's a plan. I'll call you."

"Sure. Anytime. Except for tonight, I'll be sitting with Jonas for part of the night so Danielle can get some much needed sleep. Wait, and Monday I'll be babysitting the munchkins. And Tuesday, I've got a late shift at the bookstore. Well, I'm busier than I thought."

"I've never met anyone busier."

"I know, it's the price of being in an enmeshed family. I'll leave my cell on. Please call whenever. I'll manage to find time for you. *Maybe.*" Her tone said otherwise.

He *did* like her. There was no point in denying it. He hadn't given thanks for his life in a long time, but spending the day with Aubrey and her family had inspired him. The blessing of friendship was nothing to take for granted. He popped the locks and opened the door. He'd never found it so hard to leave her before, but she stood there, blond hair rippling in the breeze, looking like everything good in the world. And it was an image that stuck with him long after he'd driven away. He couldn't explain why.

Or why he felt a little bit more like the man he used to be.

It started the instant she walked back through Katherine's front door. Her sisters were being way too sisterly, bless them. Ava was radiating joy as if she were a star shining under its own power. Katherine was looking pleased as she sliced perfect pieces of chocolate pie and slipped them onto dessert plates.

"This is super-duper!" Ava burst out as she poured iced tea into a row of tumblers. "I mean, he's so totally in love with you."

"In love with me?" That was a hoot. The last time she'd looked, "friendship" was an entire universe away from "romantic love." "You're out to lunch as usual, Ava. William doesn't see me like that at all. Trust me."

"Oh, *sure* he doesn't." She'd made up her mind and apparently nothing was going to change her mind. "Katherine, what's your verdict?"

"Well, isn't it obvious?" Katherine licked a dollop of chocolate icing from her thumb as she carried the knife to the sink. "Did he look at any of us the entire time he was here?"

"In some kind of vague way." Ava spilled tea and put down the pitcher to grab at the roll of paper towels. "I don't think he noticed much of anything with Aubrey in the room."

"At last we've found a man who can see all the lovely qualities in Aubrey the way we do."

"Enough, you two." She tried to keep it light, but the truth was, this wasn't cheerful, it wasn't fun, it wasn't true. What she'd give for their words to be true, she wasn't sure, but it would be a whole lot. What could be more wonderful than for William to love her?

Talk about impossible, though. She gulped air past the pain gathering in her chest. She was the sensible one. She had to be practical. "William is a friend, nothing more. Besides, I'm not his type, and he's not my type."

Katherine shook her head stubbornly. "Sweetie, just look at the picture he took of you."

There it was, still sitting on the counter. Okay, she wanted to read everything into it, but that would be foolish. "He's a master photographer. You know we've had e-mail bids on his work in the six figures and there's no official bidding yet. He makes everything look good in his pictures. Even me."

"No one believes you, sweetie." Katherine grabbed two loaded dessert plates and headed toward the dining room with them. "Ava, do you believe her?"

"Nope, but then she's in denial."

"No, she's in love. Look at her. She's shining."

They'd guessed? She hadn't even allowed herself to think the truth, but there it was, out in the open. She couldn't argue with them. Her feelings for William, as new and as unwanted as they were, were a fact. She could deny it all she wanted to, but it didn't change her heart.

What was she going to do now? Had William guessed, too? The phone rang, and Ava dashed to get it, leaving Aubrey alone at the island where William's picture stood, a masterpiece of light and joy. She hadn't noticed it had a title before, but there it was, like all his others. *Peter 3:5.*

It wasn't one she automatically knew. Where was Katherine's Bible? Aubrey glanced around and spotted the little flowered book bag tucked in the window seat of the casual kitchen nook, where Katherine did her daily study. What luck. Aubrey went straight to it, hardly noticing Ava's excited screeching. Their maternal grandmother was on the phone. But did that distract her?

No. The Bible's leather cover was worn smooth from use and the pages whispered open as she flipped to the Book of Peter, then the chapter and, her heart jack hammering, to the verse.

*You should be known for the beauty that comes from within, the unfading beauty of a gentle and quiet spirit, which is so precious to God.*

That was it. The final falling. She couldn't seem to stop her affection for William from intensifying. Every dream rose up from her soul, and the wish that someday, maybe, William might feel this way for her, too.

# Chapter Twelve

As she tried to get some work accomplished in her studio on her grandmother's property, the only thoughts she had were of William. He'd been stubbornly at the front of her mind since she realized she was falling in love with him. This made it impossible to concentrate properly on anything, including her work. The sketches she'd come up with for her new rain chime designs were not making her happy.

Probably because she kept glancing at her watch every two seconds. William was on his way. He was supposed to be here in a while so they could go canoeing. It seemed as if she couldn't think about anything but him. Or all the things she liked about him. It was a long, long list. So long, that she would probably sit staring into space until she was in the utter and complete dark and not even notice.

The last thing she should be doing, anyway, was daydreaming about the wonderful attributes of William Corey. She shouldn't be daydreaming at all, right? Well, she wasn't sure, since she'd never been prone to daydreaming before. She'd always been levelheaded, but she'd never been secretly in love before.

Her sisters had guessed. What if he had? That thought sent her into total panic. Probably, if he thought she'd fallen in love with him, he wouldn't be coming with a canoe and a picnic, right?

That lessened her panic, but she had a greater problem. Somehow, she had to keep her feelings for him secret. That meant, she had to keep the affection out of her voice, out of her words and expressions. While, at the same time, trying *not* to wonder if he was feeling this, too.

William. She knew he'd arrived a

moment before she heard the pad of his shoes on the cement outside. It was as if her soul turned toward him in acknowledgment. That's how deeply he affected her.

He filled the open doorway. "This is a nice place you've got here."

"It's my grandmother's property, although she doesn't spend a lot of time here anymore."

"Who keeps up the garden?"

"Spence, mostly, and I tend things when I can. Lately, it's been hit-and-miss, but I usually spend a lot of time here. Since Gran won't accept rent, I work it off unofficially."

"That doesn't surprise me." It was the only word William could think of to say. Seeing her again was like coming home. It was like watching dawn rise and knowing you had the whole sweet day ahead, full of possibilities. It felt right to walk right in, to stand beside her and look over her shoulder at her work on the long, scarred table. There was a big sketch pad and a careful row of descending-sized bowls, lake-gray and textured as if hammered pewter but, instead, it was glazed ceramics.

"From the lake," he realized.

"This is my prototype. You're early. It's only eleven-thirty. Let me close up and find my tennies." Like a morning breeze, she slipped from her stool and landed on her bare feet. She made no sound as she bent to drag a pair of pink sneakers from beneath the table. She slipped her feet into them and grabbed a baseball cap and sunglasses from the organizer against one wall.

How did he tell her that he hadn't intended to be thirty minutes early, it had just happened? Probably because he'd been eager to see her, to talk to her, simply to be with her. It was a comfort, he told himself, the same way it had been a comfort to sit with her family on Sunday. To feel as if he were a part of something again, even if on the outside looking in.

She had a nice setup here, a potter's wheel, an oven and a sink against the far wall. Wide wood-framed windows looked out at views on three of four walls, showing a riot of green garden, a long slope of meadow where quarter horses and paints grazed, and a wide span of gleaming river. But he was only noticing these things so intently because it gave him something to do besides focusing on Aubrey.

He followed her outside into the heat and brightness and wind, and it was as if she were leading him by the heart.

"You won't guess what I've got for us," she said over her shoulder as she traipsed up the pathway toward the gravel driveway where he'd parked. She stopped by the shade where a cloth-covered basket was tucked up against the outside wall of her studio.

"I picked them from Gran's garden and washed them. They should be dry and sun warmed." She knelt to peek beneath the cloth. "Yep. I hope you like berries."

"I've been known to eat my share."

"Excellent." Her smile made his soul sigh.

"Where's the launch?" He hadn't spotted it when he'd come in; mostly he'd wanted to find her first. He opened the passenger door for her and as she brushed close, bringing with her the scent of fabric softener and strawberries, his senses filled with her.

Her beauty, her gentleness, her graceful movements, her peaceful presence.

"Thanks for doing this with me," he said, his voice gruff with emotion, raw with honesty. "It means a lot to me to have you here like this."

"For me, too."

She eased onto the seat, and their gazes met. Locked. William realized he felt renewed. The morning seemed more joyful, the sun more cheerful and the wind more refreshing when he was with her. He was simply glad it was. It had been a long time coming, but he was finally out of the dark of his life, starting to live again. While he would never be the same or forget what he'd lost, it felt good to appreciate this life. This day.

This friendship.

Perfect peace. That's what it was like floating the river with William. Aubrey tried to take it all in and memorize each detail—the clear, gurgling river, the amber grasses drying on the riverbanks, the rustling cottonwoods stretching overhead and their dappled shade. But really, all of that was background. William was seated behind her on the board seat. The sun was behind them and she stayed in his broad-shouldered shadow. And felt protected.

Was she dazzled? Yes. One hundred percent.

"Look up ahead." William leaned close to speak against her ear. "The canyon's coming up around this bend."

His nearness brightened her. She squeezed her eyes shut to keep the secret love she felt down deep and hidden, where it belonged.

"Would you do me a favor?"

Anything, her heart answered with sheer devotion. Why couldn't she hold back these feelings?

"Would you mind digging into the basket? I've got my camera in there. I want to take a few shots."

"Sure."

Their fingers touched and she felt it all the way to her soul—and pretended she didn't. She tried hard to concentrate on the music of the river lulling them around a wide sweeping curve and offering an even more breathtaking view. A sweeping green meadow dotted with cheerful yellow sun-flowers, vibrant coneflowers and crimson Indian paintbrush swept up the reaching hills on either side of the river.

"Look." William eased the paddle out of the water and leaned so close she could feel his heart beat. "Up there, near that stump."

She was overwhelmed by him. So out of her realm of experience. Tender feelings kept rising up until all she could feel was joy. All around her sunlight gleamed on calm waters and smiled down on the flowers. She still didn't see what William had spotted until he brushed his hand with hers and gestured. There, barely taller than the fat seed-heavy tips of the wild grasses, was a tiny fawn. Soft and downy, the delicate creature lay perfectly still. Its soft brown coat was sprinkled with snowy-white speckles. Its dainty ears pricked in their di-rection. Big chocolate eyes studied them with innocent wonder.

Aubrey felt William behind her and heard the board seat creak with his weight as he leaned in for the shot. The man-made click of the shutter, as quiet as it was, was a shock in the peaceful lull. The fawn didn't move, but another had risen up out of the grass to stand and stare beside its twin. Identical little faces studied the intruders. William's shutter continued to click until a soft sound came from the edge of the meadow, and the fawns blurred into motion. In three bounds they were gone from sight, disappearing into the shelter of the trees.

"Breathtaking," William whispered, his camera silent.

Yes, breathtaking was the word. The connection she felt with him was not superficial, but deeper—one of the soul. She'd never felt like this before in her life. It was a terrifying combination of complete vulnerability, peaceful companionship. Being with William was like having all her best blessings rolled up into one. William was the man she'd always hoped to fall in love with—a strong, kind man who saw her, who accepted her and respected her, and who would never let her down.

She was so in love with him. And if she

wasn't careful, then it was going to show. William would know. And, what if he didn't feel this, too? What if he never would?

William panned with his camera for a few more shots but didn't take any. He studied her over the viewfinder. "Good thing I brought this. I almost left it at home."

"You got both of the fawns?"

"Yep. Talk about perfect timing, huh? You know, I'm taking pictures again."

"I noticed." There was so much she didn't dare let herself say. She held back all the feelings in her heart with every last ounce of her might. "You have to be glad to be working again."

"It's all because of you."

The ability to speak completely left her. All she could do was manage a nod. Did he know how amazing he was? Graced by light, guarded by the silent trees like loyal sentries behind him, he dazzled her. He was everything good and decent and right in a man. Everything a girl could dream of.

Everything she had ever dreamed of.

"Aubrey, you've been real quiet. Are you okay?"

She twisted around and there it was, the concern on his handsome face. Why did that make pain slice through her heart? "I'm good. It's just hot. I didn't expect it to be quite this hot."

"It's a scorcher. Want some water?" He pulled a small bottle of water out of his pack. "Here."

She reached to take it, doing her best to avoid his fingers with hers and his smile. "Just what I need. Thanks."

"Sure thing."

William eased back on the bench and watched as she took a sip of water. Having her with him today was like a gift. She improved his day. She was becoming his inspiration, apparently, since he had his camera with him again. Powerful affection filled him. Overwhelmed him. Carried him away like the current guiding them. He didn't know where this strong caring was coming from or why. Perhaps it was gratitude that she was here.

He reached for the little bucket of berries she'd brought. "Do you mind?"

"It's why I brought them."

Her smile did him in—made his world shift and blur. It was like changing a lens—there was that flash of a moment before his eyes adjusted as he brought a scene into crisp focus. When he saw clearly again, he had a handful of ripe, juicy strawberries and Aubrey bent close. Her silken strands of hair had escaped her ponytail, brushing his jaw.

He was distantly aware of the sides of the small canyon rising up around them, and the echoing sound of the water against the tall, ever-rising walls.

Concentrate on the scenery, Will, he told himself, but even his own thoughts came distantly, for there was only Aubrey. She was all he could see. Her rose-petal-soft skin and gentleness and heart. Her fingertips brushed him as she took a berry from the few in his hand. He could smell the sweet strawberry scent on the air between them and, without thought, he cupped her chin with his free hand. He'd surprised her; her violet-blue eyes widened and searched his.

Overwhelming tenderness for her pummeled him like a blow to his chest. Or maybe that was simply his heart unbreaking. Crisp, keen-edged affection overwhelmed him, pulling him along like gravity to the river. He leaned close and then closer, unable to stop this new, all-consuming feeling for her. His mouth hovered a scant inch over hers. "Okay?"

"Yes." The river's current quickened, and the moment he brushed his lips to hers, the canoe began a slow, graceful spin. Aubrey closed her eyes. This was her first real kiss, and it was perfection. His kiss was soft and reverent and real. This was real and it was happening.

He loves me, her heart whispered. Sweet devotion filled her until he was all she could see. Her head was spinning—no, that was the canoe. William broke the kiss, but neither of them moved. The canoe was drifting and scenery was going by. She had no idea what to say. Gratitude filled her when he smiled.

He poured the berries into her palm. "I think I'd better right this boat before we crash into the bank."

"Crashing would be bad." It was all she

could think of to say. She watched as he slipped the oar into the water. She should help him. She was perfectly capable of paddling, but she was frozen in place, so filled with rising hopes that she felt higher than the sun shining in the sky.

Sometimes dreams really did come true, she thought, but her cell began to ring. Here? In the canyon? Then she realized they had drifted safely through. William had straightened them out and the main country road was in sight.

Katherine's cell number was on the display, so she answered it. "Hello?"

"Jonas opened his eyes." Katherine's voice sounded rushed. "Dad said we should all get to the hospital."

That couldn't be good news. Aubrey flipped her phone shut. "I'm sorry. Jonas—"

"I heard." William's face had shuttered. For a moment, he looked as granite-hard and remote as the canyon walls, then he smiled at her, and the look he sent her was pure warmth.

How could he have done such a thing? The weight of it nearly destroyed him as he rowed back to the launch and hurried straight to the hospital. William couldn't even guess at what Aubrey was thinking of him; strain showed on her face. Of course, she had Jonas and her family on her mind, but beyond that, was she mad at him? Disappointed in him?

Why wouldn't she be? He was angry and disappointed in himself. Kissing her like that. What had he been thinking? That was the problem. He hadn't been thinking. He'd acted on pure tender feelings he didn't even know were there. He liked her, sure he did. He cared for her very much.

Maybe too much.

Now, had he ruined everything good in his life?

They were at the hospital. He swung into the half circle to let Aubrey out.

"I'll park and be up," he said, knowing it wasn't the time to say more.

"All right." She avoided his gaze.

Did he blame her? No. Not one bit. He couldn't stop the heavy weight of regret from settling on his chest like a two-hundred-pound barbell. He didn't know what to say as he watched her unlatch her seat belt and open the door. Again, she didn't look at him when she closed the door. Walking away, she seemed so somber. Alone.

No, maybe it was *his* loneliness he felt. The sobering knowledge that he'd messed up the best blessing he had in his life— Aubrey's friendship.

He parked and hiked through the echoing corridors of the hospital to the waiting room he'd visited before. He kept going over and over in his mind how he could fix this. How he could reassure Aubrey that he had nothing but respect for her and how important their friendship was to him. She was a sensible woman. She was bound to understand, right?

Right.

The moment he saw her, he could read it on her face. The news about Jonas was good. There was only relief and joy sparkling in her clear violet-blue eyes. She shone with gladness from the inside out; he could see all the love she had for her family. She was hugging an older woman, and talking with Katherine at the same time. Their excited conversation, while low, resonated through the solemn corridors like sunshine.

A sunshine that seemed to dim when Aubrey spotted him. "William."

Yeah, that's what he thought. Kissing her had been the wrong thing to do. The elation filling her up had dimmed, and his heart right along with it. Stiffly he headed in her direction. "I take it Jonas is going to be all right?"

"Danielle says he's foggy and confused, but that's not out of the ordinary. They'll know more after some testing, but he's awake and he's out of danger. He'll be able to go home."

Sometimes stories ended happily, and William was thankful that this was one of those times. "What a relief for Danielle. What about the kids?"

"Ava's fiancé, Brice, is watching them so we could all be here." She said nothing more and silence fell between them. "I'm sorry our canoe trip was cut short."

"There couldn't be a better reason."

He seemed so distant, Aubrey thought.

The hard look was back. He was stony with no hint of emotion. The tenderness she'd seen on his face, after their kiss, had faded slowly. The shadows returned to his eyes.

It *could* be because of the hospital, she realized and her heart broke for him. There was no possible way for him to be here and not to remember his losses. That had to be part of it, but she knew without words that he was moving emotionally away from her. His heart felt more and more distant from hers. She felt those shining dreams within her fade a bit.

"Are you uncomfortable here?" she finally broke the silence to ask. "We could go down to the cafeteria. Or the chapel."

"No, I just need some air." He jammed his hands into his pockets and looked over her shoulder at her family clustered together, now that Danielle had emerged from her meeting with the doctors. "You belong with your family. I'll wait for you out front."

A muscle twitched in his tensed jaw. It worried her. "I can catch a ride back with one of my sisters. I don't want you to be hurt by too many memories here."

"That's not it. Not solely." The tendons in his neck tightened. When he turned his focus on her, he could have been a stranger. His defenses had gone up and the shields around his heart. "I'm sorry about the kiss. I shouldn't have done it. I had no business—"

He fell silent, and in that silence shock washed through her like ice water. Had she heard him right? "You're sorry that you kissed me. You're *sorry*."

"You have no idea how much." William looked tortured. "It's my fault. I was overwhelmed, and I don't know what came over me."

He didn't know what had come over him? He didn't want to kiss her? Aubrey took a step back, too shocked to react or feel. One thing came through the shock clearly. He didn't love her. All this time, when she'd been falling in love with him, he had not been falling in love with her.

The first swipe of pain sliced through her heart.

He kept talking. "This is one thing you probably won't understand. What I did wasn't sensible. It wasn't planned out. I just wasn't prepared for how much your friendship means to me. How can we be friends after this?"

Friends. There was that word again. The one that slit open her unsuspecting heart like a serrated knife. The one word that she'd never known could hurt so much.

"I know this isn't the time or place to discuss this." He winced. He was clearly hurting, too. "But I can't let this go on. I'll wait for you outside. I'll take you home when you're ready. You should be with your family right now."

"Yes, sure." Too numb to move a muscle, she stood there, probably looking as foolish as her heart had been. She'd known all along that William wanted friendship. He apparently hadn't guessed her true feelings, which was a saving grace. She didn't want him to figure it out now. She gulped in air and took a shaky breath. "I think you should go home, William. I'll probably be here a long time, and I don't want you to wait. Not when it's in the high nineties outside."

"But I—"

"Goodbye, William."

For the first time in her life she didn't feel sensible. She pressed a hand over her heart, amazed that a part of her could hurt so much when there was nothing physically wrong.

Before the dam of feelings could break loose and he could see it, she turned on her heels and walked away. Leaving him standing there, alone.

The way he wanted to be.

## Chapter Thirteen

The moment she stepped through the hospital's main doors with Katherine and into the oppressive heat, she knew he was waiting for her. No matter how much she was hurting, her heart seemed to turn toward him like flowers to the sun. She looked and, sure enough, there he was, leaning against a bench in the shade. Waiting to talk about friendship with her.

No thanks. Not right now.

Katherine leaned close to speak low, so her voice wouldn't carry. "See what a fine man he is? How much he loves you? He's been waiting in the heat for two hours."

"Lucky me." The last thing she wanted to

do was face him. But she'd never been a coward. "Kath, why don't you go on without me."

"Sure, I understand. William wants to drive you. Don't forget we're meeting tonight at the dress shop. The wedding is on for sure." She was beaming as she moved away and called out hello to William.

William answered back, but he looked unreachable.

She'd lost him for good. She didn't have to be a rocket scientist to know that. She'd crossed the line in their friendship; he'd crossed that line for some unknown reason, and now they were left with goodbyes to say. She hated goodbyes.

He paced toward her, giving her the hint of a smile, instead of the full one. Even then, the impact of his half smile made her want to dream. It took all her strength to fight the wish for those dreams and impact of his nearness. But could she stop the love in her heart for him?

No. Even when there was no hope for the kind of relationship she wanted with William, she still loved him. She couldn't even keep control of her feelings. How sad was that? Since she couldn't stop her feelings, she had to at least cover them up. Keep things light and on the surface. Friendly. Maybe then this goodbye between them wouldn't hurt so much. Because she'd already decided. This had to be goodbye.

She would not settle for friendship and secretly hope for him to change his mind. This was a good theory, but in practice, she couldn't pretend. It was one thing when she hoped he might feel this way, too. But another when kissing her had filled him with regret. He saw it as something to apologize for.

It had been her first kiss. A disastrous first kiss.

Remember, keep it friendly, Aubrey. No matter how tough that is to do.

The sun was in her eyes when they met in the middle of the lush green lawn fronting the hospital. William towered above her, silhouetted against the sky in all his broad-shouldered glory like a legend of old. She stood in his shadow and felt plain and very sensible. "You didn't have to stay, William."

"I had to. I feel terrible. Your friendship is the best blessing—the only blessing—I've had in a long while. And I just messed it up. I have to know if you can forgive me. If we can go back to things being the way they were."

Oh, if only it were possible. She knew it wasn't because right here and now, standing in his presence, there was only turmoil and an unsettled feeling of hurt inside that she could not still or quiet by force or willpower. There was no longer the peaceful, safe harbor they'd found together.

No, this raw-edged ache in her heart came from being with him. This had gone well beyond simple friendship for her, and she could not turn back the clock or change the truth in her heart. It hurt too much. She knew it always would.

She steadied her voice before she answered him. "Now it's my turn to be sorry. No, I don't think we can go back to the way things were between us."

"Maybe if we give it a little time?"

"I wish it were that simple."

"Me, too." William hung his head. He

knew she was right, but he'd been hoping there was a way to salvage things. Neither of them had moved a hairbreadth closer, but he was intensely aware of her. How could he not notice the cute slope of her perfect nose? Or the porcelain-fine cut of her dear face? How she moved his spirit without saying a word?

He didn't want to be moved by her. He wanted to be Mount Everest, remote and cold and unreachable. But despair moved through him, pulling at him like a lead weight, taking him down, keeping him under. Like a drowning man, he gulped for air, but there was none. The brightness faded from the day, the light from the sky.

This was over, just like that? He squeezed his eyes shut so he wouldn't have to look at her. So she would stop having this over-whelming, unstoppable effect on him.

Be strong, William. Whatever happened, he had to keep distance between them. He had to stop his heart from this terrible thaw. He could walk away now and save himself more pain. So, why did his feet refuse to move?

"If you ever change your mind, or think you can forgive me," he found himself saying. "If you miss the company of having a riding companion—"

"I know what you're saying, and I won't change my mind. This is goodbye, William."

Don't go, he wanted to say. He needed her friendship. He needed—he didn't know what he needed or why he felt the way he did. And to tell her all of this would be too honest. Make him too vulnerable. He wanted to be glacier cold, but instead he was as warm as the sun-baked earth.

Good going, William. If he kept going like this, he was going to lose all control completely. Every last shield would be down, and then where would he be?

"I'm sure Danielle and Jonas will be in touch," she said as she moved away. "Don't forget the auction next Saturday."

"Will you be there?"

"No." She'd be helping with the paperwork before and after, but the gallery owner would handle the actual bidding. But explaining all that was more than she wanted to say to William. More than she could say.

What she had to do was to keep her dignity, to hold it all inside. She steeled her spine and tried to make her face as placid as possible, so that William had no hint of how she really felt. No hint at what was truly inside.

Tucking away her hopes, she gathered enough courage to do the right thing—walk away. After all, she'd known from the start that he wasn't looking for love. He probably never would be.

Walking away was the hardest thing she'd ever done. She was leaving forever the only man she'd ever loved. With every step across the grass she felt it more. The crash of those new, shining wishes for true love. The shatter of those dreams of loving William through a lifetime. Forever gone.

She could feel his gaze on her back as surely as the relentless beat of the sun, but the connection she'd felt with him, or maybe the tie she imagined, was no longer there. The sidewalk blurred ahead of her. She walked faster. The sooner she left William behind, the better. She didn't want him to ever guess how far she'd fallen for him. She never wanted him to know about the tears running down her cheeks, the first wave of the heartbreak to come.

She broke into an all-out run the instant she was in the parking garage, hoping to be in the privacy of Dorrie's car before the first sobs broke.

By the time William made it home, the sun was low in the sky, shining down on the proud profile of the Rockies, painting them luminescent rose and purple. The color streaked like tracer missiles across the sky. He escaped the echoing emptiness of his house, but the painful lonesomeness of it followed him out onto the back step and also, regretfully, Aubrey's words. Aubrey's pain. *No, I don't think we can go back to the way things were between us. I wish it were that simple.*

He scrubbed his face with his hands, unable to escape the image of her looking so forlorn, her face schooled to hide her emotions, unaware that it did no good. To him, she was as transparent as glass. He'd learned to read the subtle changes in her eyes and face, revealing her heart.

It hurt too much. All he could see was her hesitating before she ran away. Waiting for him to call her back. To say what she wanted to hear. To be what she needed him to be. To say the words he could not allow into his mind, his heart or his soul.

I cannot love her. Even as he willed the words to be true, he knew that they weren't. He'd done everything he could, raised every shield and used his every defense so this wouldn't happen. So he wouldn't be here right now feeling as if he'd had his chest ripped open, bleeding from the inside out. But what good did it do?

He could hold on to that truth as hard as he wanted to, but it would make no difference. It would not make the pain inside him go away. It would not make the raw, open spaces in his heart close up and heal.

Because it was no longer the truth. The one thing he'd held on to so tightly with all his white-knuckled strength had become a falsehood and, even knowing that, he could not let go of it. Could not face what the truth had become.

He did love her. What could he do about

that? He could sit here and try to hold back and change the tides of his heart.

Or he could simply wait and over time, these strong feelings for her would fade into nothing at all.

*I will not love her.*

He held on to that wish with all his inner strength and steely willpower. Although he feared it would do no good. He suspected that it was too late.

It had been a tough afternoon to get through, but she'd done it. She had her car back, her calm back and if her heart was still in a million pieces, nobody had to know. Aubrey pulled her sensible beige Toyota into the bridal shop's parking lot and recognized most of the parked cars—most of the family had beaten her here. Ava was just climbing out of her SUV.

"Hey, Aub? Are you okay?"

Aubrey startled. Her brain was foggy, but apparently she wasn't hiding her heartbreak well enough. Some things were too private to share. At least, right now. She shut her car door and studied her twin, who had strawberry icing streaked across the front of her bright yellow T-shirt. "Yeah, I'll survive."

"You don't look like it."

"It's been a long day." It was her story and she was sticking to it. She followed her twin toward the shop's front door. Everything felt like a mess—mind, body and soul. She gulped in a breath of hot, dry July air.

Pull it together, Aubrey. Somehow, she had to act as if nothing had happened, and how impossible was that? She *wasn't* all right. With so much of her heart missing, how could she ever be okay again?

But finally, there was so much to celebrate—and without worry or tragedy. This was Katherine's final fitting for her wedding. There was so much to look forward to. Their grandmother's upcoming visit. Ava's engagement. Jonas's improvement. So much to be grateful for. She would concentrate on that.

Sounded like a good plan, right? Aubrey felt a crack of pain in her soul and she sealed up her feelings. Somehow, she had to put on a smile for her family. For herself. For her dignity.

Katherine must have seen them coming because she opened the door. She looked radiant; how could she not be? She'd found the love of her life. No one deserved a good man the way Katherine did.

"Ava, you're hardly late. This is like a major miracle. A once-in-a-lifetime occurrence." Katherine held the door wider.

"A total shocker," Aubrey found herself saying, as if the day hadn't happened. As if she had a whole heart beating within her chest.

Ava sparkled as she marched to the front door of the wedding boutique. "Hey, it's not as if I'm never on time."

"Just *almost* never on time," Katherine teased. She looked beautiful, as always, in a navy knit summer top and tasteful navy shorts. Her matching flats didn't seem to actually touch the ground. She looked so happy she seemed to float.

"Ooh, look at that dress!" Ava was immediately distracted by a shop crammed full of wedding gowns. "How am I ever going to decide for my wedding? This is torture. Who knew getting married was so agonizing? Which dress? Which bridesmaids' dresses? Where, when, how, and then trying to fit everything on my poor credit card."

Aubrey hung back, letting the door close behind her, trying to put her plan in place. She swallowed hard. Just because she was surrounded by beautiful, exquisite wedding dresses simply waiting to be worn, she didn't have to be reminded that she'd dared to secretly pick out her own gown long ago.

It was still there, a princess-style satin with hand-sewn pearls. She'd never dared to let herself think of wearing it before. She'd fallen in love with it long before she'd ever met William. But now, she realized it was one of those secret dreams she'd never let herself actually picture. But it was there, still, in the pieces of her heart.

Don't think about what you lost, Aubrey.

She turned her back on the dress. On the dream. On the wish. If only she could turn her back and deny how much she'd loved him. Still hopelessly loved him.

"This way, girls!" Dorrie squeezed between rows of white satin and tulle and popped into sight. "The dresses are laid out

Everyday Blessings*

and ready. My, they're so beautiful. Aubrey, dear, are you all right?"

She suspected her stepmom had figured things out. She swallowed hard as Dorrie headed straight for her with that penetrating, motherly radar. There was no way she could hold it together if everyone knew. No, these feelings had to stay hidden for now, even if she felt so alone, without her sisters' comfort.

Aubrey forced what she hoped was a smile on her face. "I can't wait to try on my bridesmaid's dress."

"Aubrey's just had another date with William," Ava volunteered, looking even happier. "So you know she's got to be happy. William likes her."

Those words were like a knife twisting in her heart. Aubrey gasped from the pain. "N-no. You have that wrong. We're not a couple."

"Yet." Ava piped in. "You're just in the denial stage. I know. I was there a long time."

"I'm not in denial."

"Ha! That sounds like denial to me." Ava grinned. "What do you think, Katherine?"

"I think it's official."

How did she make them understand? "Oh no, you have it all wrong."

"Oh, sure we do." Ava wasn't believing a word of it.

"He's such a nice man." Katherine smiled her approval. "See? What did I tell you? Good things happen to good people."

She couldn't take it anymore. Aubrey opened her mouth to tell them the truth, but all her pain stuck in the middle of her throat. Only a squeak came out. How did she get them to change the subject? It was killing her to hear his name and to stand in this shop with happiness and the promise of wishes coming true all around her. Her heart cracked all the way down to her soul.

"You girls, look what you've done." Dorrie's scolding was loving and sympathetic as she took Aubrey by the shoulder. "Poor Aubrey is speechless. Come along and let's get these dresses on. Where is Rebecca? Is that her, driving up?"

Aubrey didn't think she'd ever been so grateful for her stepmom. Somehow, she managed to head toward the back where the dressing rooms were. She heard Ava call out, "No, that's not Becca. It's the teenager."

"How's she working out at the bakery?" Dorrie asked Ava as Aubrey ducked behind a long rack of exquisite silk dresses.

"Great," Ava said.

Aubrey spotted a chair and plopped into it. She smiled at the store worker who was prepping the changing rooms with bridesmaid's dresses in varying tones of soft pinks.

She'd never felt so alone.

## Chapter Fourteen

Aubrey couldn't remember such a bleak night. Of course, her mood might have something to do with it. She'd successfully got through the dress fitting intact. Now, she had one more errand and then she could call her day done. The first thing she was going to do was head home to her apartment, draw a bath and try to soothe away all this horrible grief. Somehow she had to figure out a way to put herself back together. Who knew love—and losing it—could hurt so much?

She pulled her car to a stop in Danielle's driveway and turned off the ignition. The headlights died, leaving such a thick darkness that it felt as if she'd been turned inside out and she were looking at the contents of her heart.

She carefully gathered the plastic-encased bridesmaid dress from the seat beside her and stepped out into the darkness. The humid puff of wind was oppressive and smelled like steam. A storm was on the way. Already the sky was endless and moonless. Clouds had blotted out the stars on her drive over, and now it was hard to make out the steps to the front door, even with the ambient light from the street and the other neighbors' houses. Danielle's windows were dark. The kitchen window, the closest window to the door, was curtained and dark, too.

Not wanting to wake the kids, Aubrey found the key on her ring and unlocked the door. Danielle knew she was coming over with the dress, but she called out softly in the entryway, not wanting to startle her. "Dani?"

"In here," came a thin reply.

Aubrey followed the sound of her sister's voice through the dark to the living room, where a small reading lamp illuminated Danielle seated in an overstuffed chair. The rest of the living room was dark and quiet, which was definitely not normal. Had something else happened when they'd been at the dress fitting, and then out to dinner? Worry ratcheted through her. "Are you all right? Jonas? He is all right?"

"Yes. I'm just tired."

Whew. Aubrey set her keys and the dress down on the couch and came farther into the room. "You look a lot more than tired."

"I think it's the letdown. I've been running on fear and adrenaline and willpower for so long, now that the crisis is over, I can't move."

"Then you don't have to. I can stay and help, if you want."

"You have done too much already, although there is one more thing. I could use a hug." Danielle stood and held out her arms. Her clothes hung on her. She'd lost so much weight. Exhaustion marked her lovely face.

Aubrey held her tight. Maybe she needed a hug, too. When she stepped back, she resolved to stay a little longer and make sure Danielle didn't need anything else. "The good news is that you can sleep all night in your own bed."

"Now that Jonas is sleeping peacefully, yes." Danielle took a step back, letting the dark take her. "It was all I could do to leave him, even when the doctors said he would be fine tonight."

"It's been a long road for you."

"Yes, but I haven't been on that road alone. How can I ever thank everybody? And you, too."

Just what I needed, Aubrey thought. A reminder of how full her life was and how blessed. "Thanks aren't necessary. Taking care of you is. Did you manage to get any supper?"

"Oh, I fed the kids some mac and cheese and nibbled on that. It was nice to be able to make their meal and give them their baths and put them to bed. Everything is going to go back to normal. And get better from here on out."

"That's what we're all praying for."

You know what? She was who she was—

sensible, practical—and she was glad for that. Perhaps she would never be adorable like her twin or classy like Katherine or truly lovely like Danielle, but Aubrey didn't mind so much about that anymore. She made a difference being who she was. After all, *someone* had to be sensible.

She took Danielle by the hand. "Let me make your favorite sandwich. We'll get food in your stomach and put you to bed. A good night's sleep will make tomorrow easier to deal with. Do you want me to stay in the guest room? I can keep an ear out for the kids."

"No, the sandwich would be enough. If you don't mind."

"Are you kidding? It's my pleasure. Oh, and before I forget the reason I came over here in the first place, here's your brides-maid's dress." Aubrey clicked on another lamp so they could both admire the exquisite gown.

Danielle sighed in admiration. "Katherine has such good taste. This is lovely."

"If you need any alterations, just give the dress lady a call. I'll put her card by the phone in the kitchen just in case." Aubrey snapped on lights and seated Danielle down at the table in the eating nook. "Here are some chips to munch on while I grill the sandwich."

"You didn't notice." Danielle sounded surprised as she tore open the new bag of Ruffles.

Aubrey knelt to drag the frying pan out of the lower cabinet. She slid it onto the stove's burner with a slight clatter. "Notice what?"

"Where I hung William's picture."

*William.* Like another blow to her heart, she almost lost her balance. She quickly grabbed onto the counter as her head began to spin. Her heart shattered all over again. The feelings she'd tucked away to deal with later rushing through her fortifications like a wall of water through a dam's concrete wall. She could feel every piece breaking. Every crack and fissure and fracture.

Why had he kissed her if he didn't love her? If he'd never loved her?

She gulped in air, refusing to cry. Knowing that it was too late. Her eyes burned, and her vision blurred. And there was Danielle at her side, reaching to pull her into a sisterly hug and wipe her tears.

It was Danielle who was taking care of her now, leading her to the table, sitting down to comfort her. "What happened with William?"

"Nothing." It was the simple, painful truth. "Nothing at all."

Danielle's voice broke with sympathy. "Oh, honey, I'm so sorry. We all had such high hopes for the two of you."

"Me, too." It hurt even worse to admit. The tears came for a second time, blurring the picture hung on the wall, where light still found it, even in the shadowed recesses of the room. An image of faith, despite the tragedy of winter's numbing cold.

She laid her head in her hands and let go of the last of her hope. The last of her hope for William's love.

It was another perfect Montana summer's day, William thought as he guided Jet through the trail's head. The air smelled sweet. Birdsong filled the vastness of his mountain paradise. There was nothing but beauty in every direction, beauty which he'd managed to capture with his camera's lens. He was back among the living. He should be happy, right?

Not. There was the truth like a big dark hole stuck in the middle of his heart, sucking at the brightness of the day and draining any chance he had for peace. It was that truth he kept doing his best to avoid, to ignore, to go on as if it didn't exist.

He was not in love with Aubrey. He didn't want to be in love with anyone.

After nearly two weeks of telling himself that, he still didn't believe it. After two weeks of pretending his life would go back to what it was before Aubrey, that hadn't happened, either. Because he wasn't the same man he'd been before. He hadn't been happy back then. He hadn't been whole. He'd been too afraid to try to live again, and it had happened anyway, the same way summer had come to the mountains, coaxing flowers to bloom and the grass to ripen and the glacier caps to melt.

What did he do now, when staying tough and ice-cold had been his only defense?

I'm not in love with her. How many times did he have to say that to himself to convince his heart? A hundred? A thousand? A million? There was only one love ever in his lifetime that had been something he couldn't get over. And it felt just like this.

The realization shook him. He was all out of excuses.

This couldn't be love he was feeling. He didn't want it to be, and that hadn't been able to change it. He'd denied it, ignored it, called it by a different name, tried to let it fade away. It was still here, a tenacious light that he could not defeat.

"Whoa, boy." They'd reached the mailbox and he eased Jet to a stop. A package was already protruding out of the box. He gave it a tug, thinking it was probably his latest online book order.

But no, the return address was from Danielle and Jonas Lowell. How about that? Curiosity got the best of him. He'd been keeping their family in his nightly prayers for a while now.

He'd heard the auction was a huge

success; it had been reported in the local paper. He hadn't had the heart to attend, although he'd been wondering how Jonas was doing. He kept hope that the state trooper would be restored to full health and be able to take his son to the upcoming county fair for his birthday. It was hard to forget the first time he'd met the little boy, for it had been the memorable evening when he'd met Aubrey.

Aubrey. Knowing her had forever changed him.

Wasn't admitting it the first step?

He tore through the tape holding the cardboard box, peeled back the top flaps and stared in disbelief. It was the ceramic bowls, in descending sizes, that he'd seen on Aubrey's worktable. Not, bowls, he corrected, her rain chimes that looked like hammered pewter. Like the lake where he'd taken her riding.

I do love her. The truth was there in his heart. But that wasn't enough. Not by a long shot. For with loving came too much risk. He didn't know if he could ever imagine risking so much again.

There was a letter, too, on Danielle's sta-
tionary. It was just a short note.

William,
   All is well here, which is a welcome
change. I picked something up at the
auction for you. An original. One of a
kind. Aubrey designed it, but didn't
have the heart to make more than this
single design. I suspect it hurts her too
much.
*Proverbs 13:12*

It hurt *him* too much. Danielle's words hit
a familiar note. So did her chosen passage.
He knew it.
   *Hope deferred makes the heart sick, but
a longing fulfilled is a tree of life.* Remembering those words made hope move
through with a powerful force.
   Aubrey. There she was in his mind's eye.
He could see, in memory, the image of her
when they'd been riding to the lake. Her slim
shadow had trailed at an angle beside him,
staying directly within his line of sight
through part of the ride. He could remember

how the sun had beat against his back and shoulder, and how the feel of being with her was like the exact peace he always found in the mountains.

He closed his eyes, and he was seeing her with his heart, riding her dainty Arabian with a born horsewoman's grace. Sitting easily and straight backed in her saddle, her smile gentle and her quiet presence infinitely precious to him. She had become his innermost dream.

How was that possible? He was a man who'd lost so many dreams that he had none left. None.

Until now.

Loving again made him too vulnerable. It was too much to risk. After surviving what he'd been through, could he put everything he was on the line and open his heart to love? To Aubrey?

He did not know if he had enough hope for that.

## Chapter Fifteen

It was another lovely Friday evening. Aubrey pulled into Danielle's driveway, leaving room for her to back her minivan out of the garage, and grabbed the big take-out bags she'd picked up on the way in. The wonderful spicy fragrance of Mr. Paco's Tacos made her stomach rumble.

At least she was starting to get her appetite back. It seemed that recovering from heartbreak was more complicated than she'd ever expected, but she was starting to feel more like herself. And surely copious amounts of nachos and Mexi-fries would help.

Before she made it halfway to the front

door, it swung open and there was Tyler in his fireman hat. He was sopping wet, as if he'd stood in a sprinkler for a full hour, and was dripping onto the entryway floor.

"Aunt Aubrey! I put out five whole fires."

"You did good today, kid."

"I know! An' we went grocery shoppin' an' a fire truck zoomed by an' Mom had to pull over and everything!"

"It's a good thing I brought extra tacos. I hear firemen get pretty hungry fighting fires."

"Yep. Did you bring Mexi-fries?" Tyler tried to peer into one of the bags.

So she gave him the lightest one, with the enormous tub of Mexi-fries. "How could I forget Mexi-fries? Go put those on the table for me, okay, tiger?"

"Okay." He marched off, leaving wet sandal prints across the kitchen floor.

Danielle came around the corner of the kitchen with Madison on her hip, saw the water marks and sighed. "It's been a busy day. I'll get that mopped up."

"No, I'll take care of it." After all, she had a flair for taking care of things. "Go have dinner at the hospital with your husband."

"Since we can't have dinner out, I'm taking dinner to him." Madison was wiggling and leaning hard against Danielle's hold on her. "No way, kiddo. I'm going to belt you into your high chair."

Madison squealed a loud protest.

"Aubrey, I've been chasing her around all day. She's discovered if she runs at full speed when I'm not paying perfect attention, I might not be able to catch up to her for a while. Oh, and she's unlocking the door, too."

"Aw, freedom. I understand." Aubrey set the restaurant bag on the table next to Tyler's bag of Mexi-fries. "I'll keep an eagle eye on her so she doesn't take off down the street."

"I have complete faith in you." Danielle stopped to kiss her kids' cheeks. "Okay, you know the drill. I rented a movie for Tyler to watch tonight—it's on the coffee table. I shouldn't be out too late."

"Take your time. I'm starting a new book tonight."

"One of those old thick ones?" Danielle smiled as she grabbed her purse and swung open the inside garage door. "I won't even tease you about that. Good night."

The door closed, and she was gone. It felt good having life back to normal. Well, almost normal, she thought, noticing William's picture on the wall.

Some things time didn't heal. She suspected the love she had for him was one of them. Neither rejection nor lost hope nor heartbreak had made a dent in that shining love.

The knock at the door had Tyler leaping up from the table before she could start the evening blessing.

"Who is it?" Tyler was all energy as she raced through the kitchen, dripping more water as he went.

"It's probably Rebecca. Maybe she forgot her key." Aubrey had half expected Rebecca to stop by at some point. They'd spent a good deal of time on the phone earlier. Things weren't going well with her boyfriend and Rebecca didn't want to spend a Friday evening alone.

"You're not Rebecca." Tyler declared once he'd yanked open the door.

"No, I'm not. Sorry, kid." That warm, cozy baritone sounded familiar.

William. She had to be hearing things. Missing him so sorely that she'd dreamed him up.

She wasn't aware of crossing the kitchen until her sneaker squeaked in a water puddle. She didn't remember reaching the door or even consider that maybe it would be best not to see William. Suddenly she was there, in front of him, gazing at him, wonderful him. So big and strong, he was all she could see. Her entire spirit brightened with joy.

Oh, Aubrey. You love this man too much. It was probably on her face. Lord knows it was a powerful light in her heart that would not fade. She tried to tuck down her feelings and manage what she hoped was a cordial— and not an adoring—smile.

She would always love him. It would hurt that he'd rejected her. But she was a sensible girl, and she could handle this. "You're looking for Danielle, right?"

"Uh, no. I came for you."

"Me?" Renewed pain cracked through her, soul deep. She thought she knew, but she had to ask. She had to hear it from his lips. "Why are you here?"

"Because I want to discuss this friendship thing. We didn't finish it that day at the hospital, and I have something to say."

She squeezed her eyes closed, trying against hope to keep the pain hidden. She feared she was failing at that, too. "No, I meant what I said. I can't go back to being friends."

"Exactly. That's what I want to talk to you about. Will you let me in?"

"You don't know how much this is hurting me. You don't know—"

"Yes, I do." He held out his hand, palm up, as if offering his heart to her like a knight of old in one of those aged, thick books she loved so well.

She'd never wanted anything more than to place her hand in his. But she could not accept what he was offering. Friendship was no longer enough. Madison chose that moment to start yelling and banging on her high-chair tray. The air conditioner kicked on, as warm air sailed into the house. Inviting him in was the practical thing to do.

She stepped back with a nod and headed straight to Madison. "Be careful of the water on the floor," she said over her shoulder and above Madison's ten-decibel-level shout for "taters."

"You look pretty busy," he said uncertainly. "I should come back at another time."

"No, say what you've come to say and then you can go." She didn't say the words unkindly.

"I need your forgiveness." William took a deep breath. This wasn't easy. He didn't know if he'd destroyed the only chance he had with her. Because he knew—soul deep—that she was his one hope for a real life. A real love. Real happiness.

"Hey, mister." Tyler skidded to a stop next to him and held up all five fingers on his left hand. "I'm gonna be this much tomorrow. We're havin' cake. Aunt Ava's making me a firehouse cake! With a truck an' a dog an' everything!"

"Happy birthday, little man." His throat

ached as he watched the kid rush the rest of the way to the table and climb into his booster seat. That must mean Jonas was well enough, maybe not to leave the hospital, but to have guests visit with cake.

Now he had to face Aubrey. He waited while she oversaw Tyler's blessing and handed out the tacos and Mexi-fries. The little girl in the high chair dug into her Tater Tots and a hot dog with gusto. They looked like happy kids. Just the way things should be. They had a happy ending. Now he was praying that there would be one for him, too.

Aubrey stopped before him, unaware that she was standing exactly where she'd been that first evening, holding a crying Madison, when he'd fallen, unknowingly, in love with her. Because he realized it now. Could see it for what it was. He didn't need the brush of evening's gentle rose light falling over her to know she was his future and his heart's reason for beating.

"You were right, Aubrey. We can't go back to being friends. I don't want to be friends."

Her eyes widened. She stood before him, so vulnerable and dear. "You don't?"

Was she really so surprised? "No. I'm in love with you. One hundred percent. Down to the soul. Forever and ever. I should have realized it. I should have—"

"You love me? That's why you're here?"

It was the hardest thing he'd ever done to see the pain in her eyes. To know his fears had done this. That's what made him take the final risk, and lay all of his heart on the line. "It's why I'm here. To ask you to forgive me. To ask if you love me like this, too."

"Forever and ever?" she asked, as if she were weighing and measuring what remained in her heart. "Down to the soul?"

He couldn't breathe or even blink. He'd never been so vulnerable.

Then she smiled. "Yes. That is exactly how I love you."

Relief left him dizzy. Until this moment he hadn't been sure. "I'm glad we have this deep love in common, too."

"This feels like a dream."

"I think it is. I found my dream, my heart, my purpose, and it's you, Aubrey."

She felt blinded by the overwhelming strength of her love for him. It grew stronger with each passing second. Each breath. Each heartbeat. Hope filled her until she couldn't speak, only feel.

She finally had her own happily-ever-after.

## Epilogue

"It's time to throw the bouquet!"

Aubrey looked up at the sound of her twin's voice. Sure enough, there was Ava on the gazebo in her grandmother's backyard. She'd seized control of one of the microphones for the string quartet to make the announcement.

"All you single ladies, line up. C'mon. Don't be shy!"

William's hand tightened around hers. "I guess that means you, technically."

"You haven't official proposed, you know."

"I was waiting for the right moment. It's hard getting you alone. You have a lot of family." He smiled wide enough that his dimples showed. "First there was Katherine's wedding shower. Then your grandmother's homecoming. And now the wedding. There hasn't been a lot of time."

"I know. It's the hazard of having a large enmeshed family."

"That happens to be the kind I like." He pressed a kiss to her cheek. "Go on. If you don't, your sister is never going to stop talking into the mike."

"It's true." She left him chuckling, but in truth, she was so happy she didn't think her slippers touched the ground as she floated toward the gazebo where Katherine had taken her flower-launching position.

He trailed after her and took a spot on the sidelines. Oh, he looked like a dream in his black tux. She stood there, oblivious to all the festive cheers and speeches, simply drinking in the sight of him. He was her own love, her true romantic hero. Each day spent with him was happier than the last. She had her best blessings in him.

"Okay!" Katherine's joyful voice vaguely pierced Aubrey's thoughts. "Is everyone ready? Catching stances, girls. Here it comes!"

Aubrey loved how the evening's sunlight seemed to find William. It caressed the strong line of his wide shoulders and high-lighted him. He was a man of such strong character and kindness, this man she would love for the rest of her life.

Something smacked her against the side of her head.

"Aubrey!" It was Ava, scolding her. "You were supposed to catch it."

"What?" Okay, she was a little preoccupied. Being in love could do that to a girl. Sure enough, Katherine's lovely bouquet was at her feet. And something was glinting there. Something tied on to the lovely pink satin ribbon.

William knelt to pick up the bouquet. The glint became princess-cut diamonds on a platinum band. "I have a question to ask you."

"How handy that you're on one knee."

"Exactly." His smile was her heaven. "Aubrey McKaslin, will you marry me?"

The cheers from her family started and so

she didn't bother saying it loud enough for everyone to hear. She leaned close to whisper, so that he could know first. "It would be an honor."

William's hand was shaking as he slipped the ring on her finger. The diamonds sparkled like all the promises he intended to make to her—and to keep.

He swung her into his arms for a romantic kiss—much to the delight of the wedding guests.

He'd found his happily-ever-after, too. He was, after all, a deeply hopeful man.

\* \* \* \* \*

*Don't miss Jillian Hart's*
*next Inspirational romance,*
*A McKASLIN HOMECOMING,*
*available July 2007 from Love Inspired.*

Dear Reader,

Thank you so much for choosing *Everyday Blessings*. I hope you enjoyed reading Aubrey and William's story as much as I did writing it. William has given up on living and on love—until Aubrey comes into his life. If you're going through a tough time, please take heart. There are so many wonderful, everyday blessings God has in store for all of us.

Please watch for sister Lauren's story, *A McKaslin Homecoming,* available next month.

Wishing you the best of blessings,

Jillian Hart

# QUESTIONS FOR DISCUSSION

1. At the beginning of the story, Aubrey believes that she's a sensible, average kind of girl. She's afraid to even think about dating. Have you ever felt this way? What does it say about Aubrey's character?

2. What is Aubrey's first impression of William? How does her impression of him change after learning his history? How does this change her feelings toward him?

3. William is able to see Aubrey's inner beauty. What does this say about his character?

4. How has William's life experience affected him? How has that kept him from trusting others? What fear keeps him from falling in love with Aubrey?

5. How is God's leading evident in their romance?

6. What does the photograph that William takes of Aubrey represent? Why does this affect her so deeply? How does this help her to come to terms with the sensible woman she is?

7. How does God guide William to hope?

8. How important are the values of family to Aubrey? How has she helped her family through hardships and how have they helped her? How important are those values to William? How does this influence their growing relationship?

9. How important are the values of compassion and service to others in this story?

10. Life is often a combination of sweet and sad. How is this theme evident in *Everyday Blessings?*